IN

TROUBLE

IN
TROUBLE

Edited by

E.F. Schraeder
&
Elaine Schleiffer

Omnium Gatherum Publishing
Los Angeles CA

Library of Congress Control Number: 2022946301

"Crawl Space" by Mary Turzillo, *Bonsai Babies*
"An Ocean Below the Surface" by Nicole M. Wolverton, *The Molotov Cocktail*
"Ten Days' Grace" by Foz Meadows, *Apex Magazine*
"Tiny Teeth" by Sarah Hans, *Pseudopod*
"Three Meetings of the Pregnant Man Support Group" by James Beamon, *Apex Magazine*
"Letter from Ohio," by Zoë Brigley, author website
"Seance for a Lover" by Marge Simon, *Victims*
"Exquisite" by Lee Murray, *Tortured Willows*, reprinted in the 2022 *Rhysling Anthology*
"The Last Clean, Bright Summer" by Livia LLewelyn, *The Monstrous*
"Damsel in Distress, Redux" by Marsheila Rockwell, *Star*Line 44.3*, Summer 2021, reprinted in the 2022 *Rhysling Anthology*
"Crime Against Nature," by Lynne Schmidt, *Trampset*

First Edition

CONTENTS

FOREWORD

By Gwendolyn Kiste

The book you're holding in your hands is a form of resistance. A way of battling back against oppression. A way of not allowing some of the most hostile voices in the U.S. to drown out our own.

We're living in a post-Roe world. This is the worst sentence I've ever had to type. At this moment, it's been almost two months since the fall of Roe vs. Wade, and while I always feared this could be a horrifyingly real possibility in America, there's still a part of me left in shock and disbelief. The part of me that was genuinely hopeful that justice and decency would prevail. Alas, as we all now know, it did not, and in this new version of reality, women, trans men, and many nonbinary people are paying the price for that injustice every single day. Even though I'm a horror writer by profession, nothing can truly prepare you for living in a country where your rights have disintegrated around you.

But as we awaken each new day in a world that has turned into a nightmarish landscape, there are still ways for us to continue to fight. An anthology like *In Trouble* gives us an outlet for our rage and our grief. The stories in this table of contents run the gamut in horror. From Livia Llewellyn's monstrous coming-of-age tale, "The Last, Clean, Bright Summer" to Michelle Renee Lane's trip gone awry in "Imposter Syndrome," and from the horrors awaiting you in 1920s America in Rebecca Rowland's "Dust to Dust" to the strange something lurking on the front stoop in EV Knight's "One Stone," there's every variety of terror tucked away in these pages and every nuance of emotion, with anguish and fear and triumph all bleeding into one. Each author featured in this book is a powerhouse, the table of contents reading like a who's who of established and rising voices within the genre. Marge Simon. Lee Murray. Sumiko Saulson. Donna J.W. Munro. Angela Yuriko Smith. This is a striking and impressive anthology for any era, every story as strong as it is uncompromising. The fact that these voices are being heard now when they're undeniably needed most only makes this book that much more important.

The world is changing rapidly around us, and for the most part, it's not changing for the better. But that doesn't mean it has to stay so treacherous and terrifying forever. We have the ability to keep going, to keep talking, to keep screaming at the top of our lungs. This vital and unforgettable anthology is an incredibly meaningful step in that direction.

Literature has always been a means of activism and revolution, and that's more pivotal to remember now than ever before. There's a sense of hope when you can make yourself heard. It's real, and it's visceral, and it's happening right now all across the country as people fight back against this tremendous loss of human rights. You're not alone. None of us are. As I read the tales featured in the pages of *In Trouble*, I was reminded just how powerful we are when we're together.

Thank you to these twenty authors for writing these ferocious and heartbreaking stories. And thank you to everyone holding this book for reading them. So long as we're in this together, then we can still move forward. And in our unity, we still have a fighting chance to create a better world.

INTRODUCTION

By E.F. Schraeder

"Some situations can't be predicted." My grandmother said this to me during the 1980s when violent pushback against Roe was making headlines. "It has to be a woman's choice." She looked out the window and into a past I knew nothing about.

Her blue eyes seemed angry and sad all at once, and I sensed she was remembering far more than she was going to share. Whatever she found herself thinking in the moments between words, I knew in my bones someone she cared about needed an abortion before it was legal.

I imagined in a blink she relived a moment that changed someone's life, sliced it into a painful before and after. Was it a friend, sister, daughter, her, or my mother? I couldn't determine. I caught myself contemplating the uncertainties and contingencies, trying to figure out an unknown chain of events. I wondered how dangerous or deadly the situation might've been for the person she so fiercely guarded in her memory. I wondered but didn't ask who or why.

It wasn't any of my business.

The personal, as they say, is political, and so too is fear.

An urgency and intimacy exists in the collected genre-bending words that follow. Readers of *In Trouble* will find other-worldly and unplanned arrivals and the problems they impose; oppressive governments and mon- strously insular communities; the kindness of hopeful would-be parents; the body horrors of experiments gone sideways; interpersonal violations; neglectful and brilliant physicians. The authors of *In Trouble* ask hard questions, examine deep vulnerabilities and complex spaces. What does it mean to have bodily autonomy or to lack it? What does it mean to shape yourself to appeal to others, including those intent on harming you? What are the violent costs of such negotiations? The calculus of lost autonomy captured in this collection functions like a prism, each author offering a distinct lens.

In Trouble was born of strife, after decades of policies chipped away access to abortion, reproductive health care, and sex education. *In Trouble* lives in the wake of the recent overturning of Roe, making the contributors' insights more important than ever; they consider interpersonal paradoxes, political hypocrisies, and the nightmarish battle between basic self-determination and social control. I hope and believe *In Trouble* challenges us to take inventory of ourselves and the world we dare to imagine, dare to create.

For the personal is political, and so too is fear. The fears that have driven political action and inaction also dwell in these works, alongside the fears that fill so many hearts as we adjust to a new landscape where laws erase the line between private medical decisions and public policy. *In Trouble* reckons with messy contexts and imagines how to respond to life's inevitable questions: what to do when things don't go according to plan; how to respond when the world doesn't work as you think it should; what else can you do; what's best for you?

To demand a specific outcome without consideration of consequence or cause undercuts a generation of laws. Only a colossal failure of empathetic imagination could lead to the arrogant assumption that strangers, lawmakers, and judges might know what's best and what circumstances appropriate to override anyone's options. And yet, here we are.

In times of turmoil and trouble, I often turn to literature, but that's not a retreat. What good can a collection of stories and poems do in the face of a terrifying supreme court decision? Literary scholars and librarians have long held optimism about the role of literature in empathy-development because readers can discover painful honesty and exposure to intimate, context-dependent problems—all framed with the safe distance of a narrative voice.

From Charlotte Perkins Gilman's shrinking room to Ursula K. LeGuin's personal statements about abortion, numerous authors have steeped themselves in the task of reimagining the limiting implications of patriarchal infrastructures and investments in power-over others. The ways in which capitalism, racism, sexism, homophobia, ableism, ethnocentrism, and bias intersect to shape access to a spectrum of issues might be missed by the reductionist misnomer of the single word "choice." Within *In Trouble,* readers will find many such alternates to consider: worlds that reflect oppressive dynamics and power structures, worlds that challenge and expose violence, worlds that examine the consequences of internalized oppression, and more.

Social history, like personal history, sometimes shimmers with the dividing line of before and after framing battleground legal victories, protests, elections, and court decisions. Now Post-Roe in the U.S., this recent bitter moment carves a wedge into and against the long arc toward justice. Social and personal histories also contain moments in life that leave an impression, teach you about the world and yourself. My opinions about reproductive justice are informed by the moments before and after personal conversations like the one I had with my grandmother, not simply led by court decisions. Personal narratives and fiction alike can illuminate possibilities that may awaken the imagination, and I'm honored to have played a small part in bringing these painful, beautiful, wise, and diverse works together.

I hope the words and worlds that follow will offer such moments of reflection for readers—moments of discomfort, awakening, and reckoning. Read with care and caution. The ever-evolving and varied voices of resistance arise from surprising places, much like my grandmother's voice, trembling in fear over what it meant to be "in trouble" as they called it in her day. How badly I wanted to know what happened, and how easily I grasped what wasn't any of my business.

CRAWL SPACE

By Mary Turzillo

When we moved into this house, there was a woman living walled up between the first floor floorboards and the basement ceiling. She said she'd been there for maybe fifteen years—hid there in the crawl space as a fifth grader, a runaway, scared to go to school without her English homework. Can you imagine what an ogre that teacher was?

Former tenant told us he heard the screams, but he was scared, so he just fed her bread and canned soup. She says her last name's Martin. Pretty common, hard to trace. Parents probably moved. We decided it would cause too much hoopla to let her out. They'd probably investigate, make it a crime scene, try to make us leave, and it's a nice house. We gave her leftovers, clothes, and an iPod, though I'm not sure she can read, and may be blind after that untreated pinkeye a few months after we moved in. Whatcha gonna do? My cats like to play with her, and now my idiot son is getting ideas. Oh well. She can't get pregnant, can she?

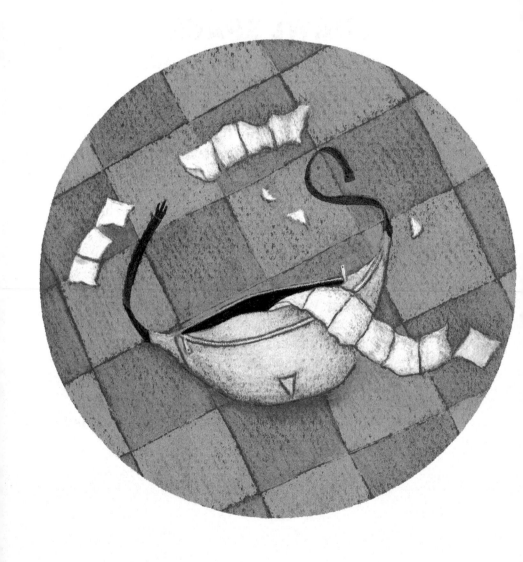

ONE STONE

By EV Knight

The thing was lying on the front stoop of her rental when Ava arrived home Sunday morning. She almost stepped on it in her rush to get away from the judgmental eyes of the cabby, who had certainly driven enough women—clad in the trappings of a "girls' night out"—home on a weekend morning to know exactly what they'd scribble in their diaries afterward. Men got away with everything and could bask in self-admiration while women, who'd done nothing different, faced glaring stares and inner degradation that came with a walk of shame.

Ava's inner monologue initially kept her from noticing the amorphous blob writhing spastically just in front of her door. Had it not moved when it did, she would have crushed it beneath her knock-off Louboutins.

"What the fuck?"

She bent down to inspect the palm-sized creature. Pale, almost transparent, gelatinous-looking flesh covered the little beastie. If there had been a beak of some sort, Ava would have guessed it a baby bird just hatched with no business flopping about on the ground. But on what she assumed to be the head, the largest of its three segments, there was only a black bulge pushed up off the side and almost bursting through the jelly-like skin. Probably an eye? If she dared touch the thing to turn it over, she suspected there would be another on the other side. The midsection offered no apparent appendages—no wings, arms, or even flippers; instead, there were just random lumps and bulges. The rest of it simply tapered away to a curved point, like a dinosaur's plump and conical tail.

As she studied the thing, it seized once into itself. The shock rocked her back, and she almost lost her balance, catching herself with her hand on the step below.

"Oh!"

"You okay there, Ava?"

Shit. Ed Whittacre, her elderly neighbor—*on his way to early Sunday services, no doubt*—would, of course, arrive just in time to gawk at her as she squatted on the stoop in her short skirt, bare legs, and heels. Clearly, she wasn't on her way to church.

She made a split-second decision and cupped the thing in her hand. It felt as sticky as it looked. She held her palm up and stood.

"Oh yeah, thanks. Just trying to save this little baby bird. Must have fallen from its nest." *There.* That had to save her some face at least.

"Oh no! Don't touch it! The mother won't want it, and it'll die. Get it back in the nest, quick!" He waved and got into his car.

Can't even do a good deed right.

It didn't matter because the thing was clearly not a bird. It would probably die because whatever mother it belonged to abandoned it on her stoop, and she was no mother.

Still, with the thing in her hand, she had to do something. It seemed cruel to leave it outside to die of exposure. At the very least, she could make it comfortable in its final hours.

By the time the thing was tucked into an old fanny pack stuffed with toilet paper, fatigue had set in. She'd gotten very little sleep, and frankly, since she had a moment to focus on herself, her hangover had caught up with her. A nap would do her good, and when she woke up and found the little thing dead, she would flush it down with the toilet paper, and that would be that.

Sleep came in fits and starts. Her legs grew restless,

followed by abdominal cramping. Ava tried to ignore it, tried hard to sleep through the worst of it, but then her mouth filled with saliva and her jaw warned her of the coming flood. She barely made it to the toilet before what little food she'd consumed the night before erupted out of her with such a force, she peed her pants, too.

Never again. She really needed to get her shit together. Clearly, a bachelor's degree in women's studies was not an open door to international diplomacy. The sickening weight of her hangover and unwarranted—yet painfully present—shame was her wake-up call.

She brushed her teeth, trying not to gag, then showered. The previous night's shenanigans left her raw, and when she wiped, there was a little pink. Ava sighed. It was a fun night, though, even if she had no intention of seeing or dating Todd again. She'd just have to accept it as the grand finale of her youth, and now it was time to buckle down and focus on her career. She intended to do great things in this world, and she didn't need a relationship holding her back.

The stink rushed at her when she opened her bedroom door, sending her right back to her knees in front of the toilet. There was nothing left inside her, but it hurt just the same.

Pulling her shirt up over her nose and breathing slowly, she padded down the hall to the kitchen, where the smell seemed to be at its strongest. The empty fanny pack lay on the floor beside the island, where she'd left it. Beyond it, closer to the stove, was the Lovecraftian thing—not only was it NOT dead, but it had, in that short time, grown to the size of a dachshund puppy. The black domes had broken through the sticky membrane, protruding like obsidian egg yolks, just waiting to be dipped into. Its head had grown larger and more rectangular, jutting out away from its grub-like body, from which five tentacular appendages erupted. Like a tadpole evolving into a frog, only the tail seemed to be regressing.

"Ugh."

And it stunk. Like old hamburger, soured blood, and dead meat left raw for far too long. But this...whatever... was not dead and rotting. Oh, no. It was very much alive.

The thing wriggled itself around to face (*is that a face?*) Ava, and grunted faintly, just loud enough so that she knew it came from the breathing chunk of writhing flesh on her kitchen floor.

"No. No, I'm sorry, but I can't do this. You have to go." Ava grabbed the strewn tissue and scooped the thing up with both hands. It hung boneless and weak as she carried it out the back door and through the yard. Still unable to be savagely cruel, she laid it rather than dropping it at the base of the hedges along the farthest edge of her yard.

It made no further grunting protests, and if it watched her go with its demonic egg yolk eyes, she didn't know, because Ava never looked back.

She slept better that night, although the nausea sent her to bed with an empty stomach, having been unable to keep anything down the rest of the day. The fresh breeze from the open windows helped to air out the odor left behind by the thing-turned-monstrosity.

At two in the morning, a dull but persistent ache in her midsection woke her. The added weight on her abdomen quickly brought to mind Fuseli's *The Nightmare,* so for a moment, Ava suspected she was experiencing the same disorder suffered by the subject of the painting—sleep paralysis. That wasn't it, though, after the fact, she wished it were. Ava could move without difficulty. She turned on the lamp beside her bed.

The thing was back, and its tentacles had grown longer—or at least four of the five had. She couldn't see the fifth, as it was currently buried deep beneath the skin of her belly, siphoning, feeding, sucking away her insides. *The fucking thing is a parasite!*

Ava grabbed it around its thick, fatty neck and threw it off her. The sickening pull as its fleshy appendage slithered out of her caused her to wretch and cough. *I've gotta kill it. Stomp it to death or something.* She could not imagine how the hell it got back in her house in the first place; it didn't even have legs.

Okay, stomping it is out of the question.

It was puppy-sized. Yet somehow without bones—still. The thing was nasty and tacky and semi-translucent. Since she had last seen it, a network of blood vessels had developed beneath its strange aspic-looking flesh. It also had a heart, and as it beat, it actually pushed against the underbelly, causing a rhythmic tick, tick, tick each time the skin touched her hard wood floor then pulled away again.

"You gotta go," she declared.

She would not—couldn't—touch it. Instead, she got some kitchen tongs, which smooshed into its sides while she carried it outside like a thick slab of raw steak. This time, she *did* drop it *and* kicked it. Shivering in disgust, she decided to bury the thing. Yes, burying something alive might be a terrible, horrific act and utterly unlike Ava, but...

She touched the small, surprisingly painless defect in her flesh just to the left of her belly button. *Ugh.* The thing was dangerous and needed to die. She supposed, besides poison, this was the epitome of a coward's version of murder, but she thought she could live with that.

Ava was exhausted when the deed was done. A quick shower, some antibiotic ointment, and a bandage covered the finger-sized hole in her gut. She used an old towel to cover the spot on the floor where the creature landed, planning to scrub it when she awoke at a more reasonable hour.

Too sick to leave home, Ava called off work Monday and Tuesday. She wasn't vomiting as much as on Sunday, but the nausea persisted, and she had no appetite. Every time she even thought about trying to eat, the memory of the jelly monster's stink or the sensation of pulling it out would hit her again, and she couldn't do it. For whatever reason, the only things she could keep down were slushies and pickles. Clearly, there was more going on than a hangover.

On Friday, Ava had a ticket to hear Gloria Allred speak at her university, but her nausea and fatigue were just too great. She spent the evening in sweats, binging Netflix, and sipping peppermint tea. Eventually, she fell asleep on the couch during episode eight of *Mind Hunter*.

A tooth hit her lip as vomit erupted from her belly. She watched it bounce off the side of the porcelain bowl while her tongue frantically searched and subsequently found the swollen, bloody womb where it once lived.

"No!"

Bits of crumbled teeth sputtered out like cracker crumbs. She reached up, cupping her mouth with her hand. Running to the sink, Ava leaned into the large, well-lit mirror and smiled a chimpanzee grin. The remainder of her dentition tumbled into the sink like dominoes.

She startled awake.

For a moment, Ava didn't know where she was, or even *when* she was. The disorientation dizzied her. Remembering her dream, she made her way, slow and unbalanced, to the bathroom. In the mirror, after determining that her teeth were all still in their proper places, she watched herself undress, aware of the sickly hue of her skin and the prominence of her collarbones. She'd always been thin, naturally athletic, and not attracted to the sweets and treats that brought on the freshman fifteen all her friends were still working hard to remove. One week of a GI bug had certainly taken its toll.

Completely naked, it really showed, her sunken belly with its curling bandage over the red wound and—wait, was that another spot just to the side of it? She inspected, running her fingers over the reverse braille. Another spot! Had the thing come back?

"No fucking way."

She'd buried it—maybe not a full six feet underground, but enough so that little boneless piglet should not have been able to dig itself back out, let alone get in her freaking house!

Ava showered, the hot water leaving her breathless and weak. She knew she should try to eat something before trying to find something to kill the little blood-sucking menace. Ideas and possible methods of monster murder ran through her head, giving her the energy needed to get dried, dressed, and make some tea and toast.

Her cell phone was dead, which was odd, as the battery typically lasted a couple of days with Ava's typical use. She scooped it up off the coffee table and plugged it in at the kitchen table while waiting for her toast to pop.

Her stomach accepted sips of tea but sent flashing warning signs to her salivary glands and gag reflex with each piece of toast she attempted to chew and swallow. Giving up on solid food, she picked up her tea and was just about to head back to the couch for the rest of *Mind Hunter* when her phone charged enough to alert her to multiple missed calls and voicemails.

What the hell? Is it Armageddon or something?

As she listened to the voicemails, Ava began to wish it was the end of the world. Nothing made sense, and her heart beat way too hard for the little energy stores she had to offer it.

"Hi Ava, this is Melody. You're scheduled to work today. It's about twenty after nine. Give me a call, please."

The rest were some form of the same message. Most from Melody, one from her mom, who was her emergency contact person—Ava had no idea they actually ever used those employee forms or even kept them, but they must have—and the last one stated she was currently six hours late for work, and Melody was going to have the police do a wellness check.

None of this made sense. It was Saturday, not Monday. She worked as a loan officer at a bank, and the bank only had drive-thru hours on Saturdays. She checked the time—3:15 p.m....on Monday! How? She'd just missed Melody's last call. She punched the green telephone icon.

"Ava? Oh my God, I was just dialing 911. Are you okay? What's going on?"

This is good. She doesn't sound mad at all, so it's salvageable.

"Honestly, Mel, I haven't felt well all week. You know I took those two days off, and I should have gone to the doctor, but I thought it was just a little bug. I honestly fell asleep on the couch and somehow just slept through the day." Melody did not need to know that Ava had actually slept through two and a half days—who was counting anyway?

"Oh, Ava. Something is terribly wrong. That's not like you at all. Call the doctor right now and make an appointment. Don't come back to work until you've seen her."

Ava chewed her lip before answering. "Yes, I will. I was going to right away, but then thought I better call you first."

"You might want to call your mom, too. I'm afraid I got her a little worked up. I was just so worried about you. You're usually so responsible."

Yes, she was...usually. She was beginning to wonder if she'd been drugged last weekend. Maybe the marks on her belly were just hickeys, and that thing was an hallucination brought on by drug residue in her system? She really didn't know Todd all that well. Had met him, what? Twice before their little drunken tryst? Maybe he tossed a roofie in her drink or something, and she was having a very prolonged reaction to it.

She carried her tea to the couch. Calling her mother would be a "sit down somewhere comfy" ordeal. She set her tea down and pushed the cushions back into their "salesfloor position" rather than the "a hobo slept here" disarray. Grabbing the throw blanket with the intent to fold it properly and throw it over the back of the couch, she gasped.

Lying, curled up into the fetal position, was the Thing, now the size of a full-size wiener dog. Its flesh looked more "fleshy," more opaque. Traces of blue lines ran across its underbelly, but she couldn't see its heart, nor did it look sticky anymore. She would describe it as vampire flesh—that semilucent, deathly pale look. Vampire was a good description for it, given that it did in fact penetrate her body and suck away her life force. She shivered. Its appendages were tucked in tight against it—*a Thing-loaf*— and she couldn't make out the changes to its face past the bulbous forehead at the top of its hyperflexed head. She took several pictures of it with her phone—evidence the Thing existed and that she was not, in fact, crazy.

"Okay. Okay," she said to calm herself. But she kept the volume of it down so as not to wake it. "You have to die. You're fucking up my health, my body, my life. You can't be here."

Forgetting her mom, forgetting the doctor, forgetting the fact that she hadn't eaten anything of substance for a week, Ava drove to the hardware store and marched right up to customer service.

She held the picture up to the older gentleman manning the counter.

"I need to kill this...whatever it is. What should I use?"

He took the phone and put on the glasses hanging around his neck. Ava watched him consider it.

"Why d'you want to kill it?"

"Does it matter? Because it's making me sick, because it's feeding off me, and frankly, because I don't want it."

"Cute little thing," he said, as if considering, and then handed the phone back. "I'm not comfortable with you killing it. I can't help you."

"What?" Ava was already out of breath from the effort of getting to the store, so she wasn't physically capable of having an argument with the old man. "It's not really up to you. It's my life, and I don't want it. Look what it is doing to me!" Without thinking about where she was, she lifted her shirt and exposed her abdomen. She pointed to the little red bullseyes on her belly. "It has tentacles, and they burrow inside of me and suck my blood or something. I'm sick, I can't eat, I'm missing work, and I'm losing weight. Please."

A crowd had started to gather. A hand fell on Ava's arm. "Honey, what's wrong?" It was Mrs. Whittacre, Ed's wife. Ava didn't know her first name; the old woman rarely spoke to her or even left the house. She reached out and tilted the phone in Ava's hand to better see the picture. "Oh my goodness, what a sweet little thing!"

"She wants to kill it," the unhelpful old man interjected.

Ava glared at him.

"What? Whyever would you do that? Look at it!"

Ava had looked at it and smelled it and, dear God, fed it. What were these people seeing that she wasn't? While Ava worked on shutting her mouth, Mrs. Whittacre began passing Ava's phone around to all the lookie-loos who'd come over to put their two cents into Ava's business.

She snatched her phone back away from the person currently cooing at how cute the thing was. "I'm going to kill it. It's ruining my life. It's not your business. It's mine. If no one here is going to help, I'll go somewhere else." She stomped out of the store.

It took all of her strength to leave the store. *Nothing else to do but go home.* Go home, and shut herself up in her room, where Thing couldn't get to her, and rest. When she felt better, she would figure out what to do. She'd find someone who could or would help her.

Ava didn't have the energy to explain the situation to her mother; instead, she assured her she was just dealing with a virus.

"No need to worry, Mom. I'm fine. Just a little rest, and

I'll be good. I'll call you soon." She hung up and fell back asleep.

The doorbell woke her up. She checked her phone, fearful of having lost more days, and was reassured to find it was still Monday. She padded down the hall, using the walls for balance as she fought off unconsciousness that threatened to bring a black curtain over her vision with every step.

No one stood at the peephole, so Ava assumed it had been a delivery driver letting her know her package arrived. Although, for the life of her, she could not recall ordering anything. Upon opening the door, she found it was, in fact, a delivery, just nothing she wanted or had asked for. Two large grocery bags filled with dog and cat treats, toys, and food dishes flanked a large brown pet bed. There was a ribbon and card on the bed. She plucked it away and opened it.

Ava,

We want to help you so that you don't feel the need to kill one of God's creatures. You were chosen for this miracle, and you must remember that the Lord works in mysterious ways. Please reconsider. We're praying you'll make the right decision.

Your friends at the Church of Christ.

"Seriously? Fuck off!" Ava kicked the gifts off her stoop and onto the yard. She would have carried them straight to the curb, but she had nothing left. She needed to eat, she had to drink, or else she was going to die, with Thing lurking around somewhere just waiting to feed off her again. She wouldn't give it the satisfaction.

Back inside, she sipped the cold tea she'd left on the

coffee table and contemplated possible food. Saltines, peanuts, oatmeal, PB and J, pancakes, eggs, bananas, rice—the inventory of the kitchen was a list of futility. Nothing sounded edible; nothing even sounded remotely doable. She decided a banana and saltines would be the best option, as they required no preparation.

Could teeth actually hurt? Because it hurt her teeth to chew the crackers. When she bit into the banana, she noted a bloody smear across the bite marks.

"Well, shit, my teeth *are* falling out." The thought shouldn't have been funny, but it was, so she giggled. The image of Jeff Goldblum in the movie *The Fly* collecting body parts in cups in his bathroom made her laugh even harder. "If I have to start vomiting on my food just to get it down, I'll skip the rest and shoot myself, thank you very much."

"Oh, fuck." She began to cry.

The week brought more changes—none of them good. She couldn't get an appointment until the following week. Melinda insisted she take a two-week leave of absence. Ed and his wife, Maggie, checked in on her multiple times. Ed brought in all the things she'd kicked off the porch. Maggie brought homemade chicken noodle soup that, to Ava, smelled like Thing, so it went down the disposal after they left. It seemed they were less interested in Ava's well-being and more so checking in on the viability of Thing, which seemed to be hibernating on her couch. But Ava knew, based on the increasing number of swollen, red punctures on her belly, it was very much awake and alive.

Her skin broke out in pimples and boils. Maggie asked her if she was "taking the meth" and had the audacity to look around her kitchen and living room as if searching for drugs—anything to explain why her young neighbor showed no interest in the creature who'd taken up residence in her home.

Bananas and crackers ran low. No one brought her any more to help her keep from starving, but bags of dog and cat food—and once bird food—were constantly left on her porch with notes from the church reminding her she was a terrible person and how they were praying for her. She tried Instacart once and ordered rat poison, but someone took the bags away before she could shuffle to the door to get them.

After that, she deadbolted the door and no longer answered Ed and Maggie's knocks. That was when the picketing started. There were no more gifts left at the door, no more soup, no more polite knocks. Instead, it seemed the entire Church of Christ began holding daily services on her front lawn. Many parishioners carried signs that said "Killer!" or "All Life is Precious!" or "Selfish Whore." All of it confused Ava, since she hadn't killed anything, and it seemed that Thing was killing her.

But the church didn't see it that way.

On Thursday, she tried to call an exterminator. Not because she'd decided to live out the destiny set forth on the picket signs. No, it was how she awakened that morning. Her breasts ached and her stomach itched, and she felt as if she couldn't breathe. She opened her eyes to find Thing, now the same shade of flesh as her own, no longer see-through at all, lay on top of her. Its thickened, ropey, center proboscis undulated as it pulled the lifeforce from her center, where it was firmly embedded, and siphoned what little reserve she still had into its own gut. But that wasn't the worst of it. No. Not by a long shot. The worst was its plump, rose-red facial sphincter that suckled at her breast. Thing's head writhed in ecstatic pleasure as it fed on her. This humanoid leech creature had grown to the size of a small basset hound.

Thing had taken all her strength, so despite her horror, she could not push it off. She managed to pull herself up and off the side of the bed, so they both fell to the floor with a thud. The fall detached its lips from her breast, but the fleshy cable between their guts was much too sturdy, so she had no choice but to drag Thing behind her as she crawled to the bathroom to vomit.

In the toilet, globs of tenacious mucus clung to the sides of the bowl. Ava was so disgusted by the sight that she backed away, only to vomit onto the floor. What landed on the cool linoleum looked like coffee grounds brewing in a vat of blood rather than water. Thing flung its cartilaginous appendages in an effort to scoot its body toward her pile of sick. It then sucked it up with the same mouth that only moments ago suckled her left breast.

Her scream sounded so weak, so quiet, Ava knew no one would hear her. The day before, she'd looked up a number for a pest removal service and intended to call, but she fell asleep before she was able. *My last chance...* or maybe it was too late for her anyway? But Thing would not beat her. It would not gain life from the loss of hers. No matter what sort of gift from God anyone else seemed to think it was, Ava knew—she'd known from the start—it would end this way if she let it get this far, yet somehow it had—and here they were.

Thankfully, Thing did not make her drag it everywhere she tried to go. It wriggled about almost joyfully behind her, following her like a puppy. It was no hardship for the creature to keep up with her, as Ava had been reduced to crawling, having no strength left to walk.

Wouldn't Maggie and her cronies love to see this.

When the "Pest-U-Less" man arrived, he never made it to the door. The protestors yelled profanities and threw clumps of dirt and rocks at him. Ava opened the door as far as the chain-lock would allow, hoping to offer him a safe haven, but he ran back to the truck and left before she could stop him.

She watched him drive away before breaking down in sobs. Thing snuggled up against her leg, rooting around like some blind newborn creature seeking sustenance. Ava's last moments came with the realization that Thing had found her breast again and latched. She was too weak to feel disgust, too weak to breathe, and soon after that, her weakened heart ceased to beat.

No one in the yard came to help. No one called for help. It was all part of God's plan, after all, or perhaps it was God's punishment for Ava's refusal to accept His gift. With no further reason to picket or protest, they packed up their signs and moved on.

Thing watched them go with its big black eyes.

When the flow stopped, it broke its seal on Ava's breast. When the blood clotted off, it pulled its feeder out as well. There, in front of the small opening to the outside world, it sat, waiting patiently for the others to come back with more food, warmth, care.

And it waited.

And waited.

No one came. No one left gifts of food for a creature no longer connected to another. No one cared to feed it or hold it or offer it protection. Thing, in the very last sad moments of its very short life, wished Ava *had* crushed it that very first day on the step. Back before it knew of life, before it knew pain and loneliness and want.

And then there was nothing.

AN OCEAN BELOW THE SURFACE

By Nicole M. Wolverton

It started with the very tip of Mamie's big toe—just a dot. A bold blue pinpoint mark that hadn't been there the day before. She tried to scrub it off, the soft nap of a washcloth giving way to the bristles of a nail brush, but it didn't matter; it didn't want to come off.

The second day, the dot grew larger. Instead of a tiny mark that looked as though someone had poked her with a pen, it was the size of a dime. The day after that, the size of a quarter, and her toenail turned blue.

Her doctor stood and stared, cocking his head this way and that. "And you're sure it won't wash off?"

"I tried," she said, thinking about trying scouring powder and a steel wool pad when she got home.

"Well." He scratched his head, "It could—have you eaten silver lately?"

"What? No."

"Maybe it's your diet."

And that was the extent of her doctor's helpful suggestions. He sent her to a dermatologist, a skinny lady with green eyes who asked her the same questions. By that time, Mamie's entire foot was blue.

Every day, some new part of her turned the blue of summer skies. She began to imagine she could see fluffy white clouds floating over her cobalt shins and azure belly.

Giant brown hawks swooped over her sapphire forearms, and pretty red cardinals darted down at her ultramarine belly button.

Weeks after that, she detected a pirate ship sailing across the electric sea of her upper thigh. The captain waved to her and steered on toward the cape of her left hip.

Mamie took to wearing short skirts and low-cut shirts when she went out of the house to show off the hue of her skin, hoping someone else could see the action movie playing out across her body. People looked, wondering, and pointing, but no one ever stopped her to say, "Miss, a dolphin is swimming in your clavicle."

Eight months after the bold blue pinpoint appeared on her toe, a miraculous thing happened: the waves began to recede. At first, it seemed like a good thing. The stain hadn't reached her face yet. She hadn't been looking forward to the tides on her cheeks calling to the moon. But then her skin parched and cracked as the color faded back to her normal paleness.

Within weeks, her skin was littered with the carcasses of dead fish.

"Can't you do something?" she asked the dermatologist, her voice frantic and frightened as she scratched at the crevices that had opened up on the desiccated flat of her bicep.

The doctor tried not to look alarmed as she smoothed moisturizer onto Mamie. Something wriggled beneath her touch.

She pulled her hand away. A lake trout flopped in her palm, gasping for air.

MUTATIO

By Querus Abuttu

From the Journal of Dr. Ellis Evita Foster July 4, 2035:

What price sacrifice? We do not admire the human who runs to survive another day.

We value the one who leaps in and sacrifices their life so others may live. We revere the one with no other thought than by dying they help others continue to connect with each other in this crazy world where time is limited, where death stalks each of us with every breath— where moments of happiness are unappreciated while moments of suffering seem to last forever. In that second of their sacrifice, there is no prize, no reward, no statue of respect or building to receive in their honor as they pass through the gates of death. Sacrifice itself is its own reward. Many of us wish for that strength of self-sacrifice, but when that moment comes, few are made of the mettle required to step up and finish the game.

We were just in our twenties when the repeal of Roe versus Wade happened, and after that, we battled the outcome, marched the streets, but things got worse. Much worse. The Far Right took over and started making even more laws that reversed women's and gay rights. Laws were passed that made my marriage to Jade once again illegal. We didn't think that could ever happen, but it did.

In our quiet home in Virginia, men in a pickup truck

stormed our home, vandalized it, raped us both, and said they did it because we were "useless lesbos."

"Maybe now that you know real men, you'll get over being with cunts," one of them taunted before they left.

I "got lucky," if you call it that, and dodged a bullet. Jade found out she was pregnant five weeks later, even though we'd washed our bodies outside and in. Oh, we knew about Rape Crisis Centers, but they didn't provide emergency contraception anymore, and our relationship was illegal, so we lived in fear. How could we prosecute men that the government supported?

Friends of ours started calling us with their own horror stories. Beatings, rapes, and sometimes murders.

"You have to do something, El." Jade's face looked up at mine, tender yet broken inside. She was a psychologist and knew we needed to face this. "You're a scientist. You cannot let them win this war."

She touched her belly as she said those words. Tears trailed down her cheeks. My heart shredded, thinking of both of us allowing—growing—this result of violence—a life that would always remind us of hatred and our fight. We had friends who could help us abort this horror in secret. But what would that do? Perpetuate secrecy. Hide our struggle. And there were millions of women who did not have that option.

Instead, we decided to make this unwanted pregnancy a symbol of our oppression as it grew inside my wife. "See what they've done to us," this symbol would say. "See the choices they've forced upon us!" it would cry. We didn't consider the effects those choices would have on everything later.

The next morning, I contacted close friends and colleagues in the biomedical sciences to float my ideas. I pulled research papers and consulted with experts in nanotechnology.

The Director of the Women's Right to Choose, or WORTOC, called me the day after that. I'd met Ms. Janet

Sullivan at the World Science Fair a few years ago during one of my presentations on genomics.

"Dr. Foster, I understand you have some ideas that can give us an edge in solving our problem," she launched with no preamble. "Some of them unusual."

"Yes, ma'am," I responded, not elaborating.

"I'll send some Sisters to help you." (That's what they called their members.) "Let them know what you need," she continued. "We don't have a lot of funds, but we can supply meals and daily items like paper towels. In return, I want a full report each week on how things are going."

So, I had my first sponsor.

There was only one way this would really work, though. We needed a location to perform research and substantial funding. My friends donated some funds but nowhere near enough. The only place I could obtain what I needed was the one place I didn't want to go.

I hadn't seen my parents since I'd graduated from Berkeley. They didn't see me get my master's or PhD They didn't see me get married. They were politically conservative, but my mother always believed a woman's body was her own, even though she was Catholic. My father was a Southern Baptist. To this day, I still don't understand how their marriage worked.

Their two-story white house stood on a hill overlooking green sweeping fields of old plantation land. I insisted that Jade come with me. Without her, my plea for help wasn't going to work. It was late March on a Saturday afternoon. Football season was over, and gardening season wasn't in full swing yet. Cherry blossoms burst forth in their glorious pink, and the air was crisp and sweet. My parents hadn't started fixing dinner. My timing was just right. Mother answered the door, a dishtowel in hand. She was drying a green ceramic mixing bowl.

Mother looked just as I remembered. She was a woman who never seemed to age. Those silver swirls still swept gracefully on top of her head, her thick glasses maybe a bit thicker now. And her face—well, it was not much more lined than the day she and my father declared that if a woman was my chosen life partner, then I was no longer part of the family. Maybe I'd hoped that rigid thinking and an immovable mind would make her body wrinkle like an ancient apple, but no, she was still beautiful to me. And the moment her gaze took me in, I saw immediate regret for the years we'd stayed apart. The bowl fell from her hands and shattered, but we paid no attention as we hugged, clung to each other, and cried. As always, she smelled of Oil of Olay.

Jade hung back.

My father stomped in. "What Sam Hill...?" He stopped. Mother turned toward him, still holding me. I couldn't see her face, but I looked at him. There was the same red-checkered flannel shirt he always wore. He used suspenders to hold up his jeans now. I noticed when he spotted Jade over my shoulder.

Oh, no, I thought. I felt the thunder coming—lightning slashing. Pops was renowned for his temper. When he got started, he was angrier than Moses coming down from the mountain dashing stone tablets—handwritten by God—to the ground. I braced for the harsh words.

"Well," I heard him say. "Bring 'em in, Ann."

I don't know what happened to my parents over the years, but seeing me again did something to make them rethink priorities. We sat on their sofas in the living room, and Mother listened to our story. She sat next to Jade and even asked if she could touch her belly for a moment. Pops watched the TV—though I caught his eyes flicker toward us now and then. He still wore his tidy haircut from the days of working on the Hill, though he never needed to work since the discovery of a gold vein in one of the caverns on his land. He just liked being in the mix back then.

"And so, we are in need of a place to build a research lab underground," I said. "Someplace the government wouldn't know where to look. I know Pops got the old mine south of here..." My "southern speak" always returned when I came home. I caught Jade's slight twitch at the corner of her mouth.

Yes, Jade, ha ha, funny.

The old man surprised the hell out of me, although he shot a dagger-look at Jade, then a soft look at her belly, before he said, "I got you something better."

He hefted his body up, walked over to a far wall, and opened his desk. There was a map and blueprints he motioned me to come see. Turned out that during the years of Operation Iraqi Freedom and then Operation Enduring Freedom—which questionably resulted in anyone's freedom—and then when Vladimir Putin got a burr up his ass and started attacking the Ukraine in 2022, Pops was building an underground bunker with tunnels big enough to run vehicles through and rooms secure enough for sheltering people.

"You'll have to make it research worthy, but you wanted 'underground and secure.' It's there. It's ready."

I wanted to rage and ask him why now? We'd wasted years being so angry at each other. Maybe all he was thinking of was the little grandchild inside of Jade. It wasn't really his—strange, I know—but maybe he thought of it that way. When I looked at Jade, into those warm hazel eyes, I didn't dare go off. I swallowed my pride.

There was no help for it, though. I had to ask. "Pops, you spent millions building that place. Why let me use it now?"

"Pshaw," he said. "It was a project. Something fun. I figured if it ever looked like the real Armageddon or some such shit, your mother and I would have a place to shelter. Bring friends. Hang out. Live for a while. Like that movie—what was it, Ann?"

"Blast from the Past, Ray." Mother smiled at him, the corners of her eyes crinkling, but she sobered. "What he isn't telling you is that he nearly died a month ago. We wanted to call you and didn't know where to begin at first.

Your father had a heart attack. Ended up needing a triple bypass, and well—"

"My worldview changed a bit," Pops said. "I still don't hold with the life you chose, but..."

It was clear he couldn't finish his sentence. He cleared his throat and looked at the ceiling.

I glanced over at Jade. Her eyes seemed to say *just breathe*. I embraced him. "Thank you, Pops. And if Armageddon does come and you want shelter, please don't hesitate."

He hobbled over to Mother, who stood up from the sofa. He squeezed her tight. "Little girl, that place ain't the only egg in my basket." Without looking at Jade, he nodded toward her. "Let us know how our grandbaby turns out."

Mother gave Jade a hand to stand up and wrapped my wife in a warm embrace. She slipped something into her hand that I couldn't see. Jade never showed me what Mother gave her.

And so I gathered my army. I called every friend I'd studied with at Berkeley and UCSF. I contacted fellow professors at Yale and Harvard. Geneticists, biochemists, and engineers I'd written papers with. They texted their friends at prestigious labs and research centers about our cause and advised each other to make purchases of burner phones to call my central number. For those who called me, I pitched my proposal and a meeting date.

Word of our efforts spread in a week. I had a bunker, starting cash Pops provided, and donations from friends. The next hurdle wouldn't be easy.

I had to separate those dedicated to the cause from those who were not. It was not just a question of ethics anymore, because ethics depended on which side of the dividing line they stood.

Richmond, Virginia, was the best location for a potential research team to meet. It was on a major interstate, not as dangerous as DC or as rural as Charlottesville, which would also be too close to the bunker location. I selected a hotel, and at the appointed time stood in front of my colleagues—peers, former professors, friends—feeling like I was ready to do a TED Talk.

"A woman's right to choose what happens to her body the moment a fertilized egg implants in her uterus is now extinct," I announced.

On screen, I showed scenes of violence much like what Jade and I had suffered, like my friends suffered. I clicked to the dividing cells of the egg after fertilization and then clicked to show implantation in the uterus, then showed a pregnant fourteen-year-old girl next to a pregnant forty-five-year-old woman. I clicked again to show a woman standing with ten children, clearly her own, all living in poverty.

"Laws passed in our states and in our nation make abortion a crime. Even Plan B is unavailable because of new legislation. Same-sex marriages are now illegal. Our very freedoms are slipping through our hands." My next slide showed people trying to hang onto a rope, but they were falling—the rope coated with oil.

"I propose we fight back." I clicked and showed a picture of CRISPR-CAS9, a genome editing tool that essentially cuts out a piece of a genome and replaces it with another. "You all know what this is." I went to the next slide. "And you all know who he is." I showed a photo of the Chinese biophysicist, Dr. He Jiankui. "And the results of what he did." The next photo of his twin girls. In 2018, he genetically altered the genes of his girls to be genetically resistant to HIV.

The room, which had been filled with small noises and polite whispers, became very quiet.

"Imagine if the human body were provided selective biological weapons." My next photo showed a collage of acid-slitting insects. "Such that it could decide when to use those weapons to defend itself."

Out of the corner of my eye, I saw two individuals pack up their items and leave, and then a friend of mine blatantly shook her head in front of me, threw her tote over her shoulder, and exited.

"What if a woman's body could be designed to automatically choose if it accepted a mate? Or if she wanted to be pregnant?"

More scientists walked out. Still, I pressed on. I explained the future human selection process, human trials, and the length of time expected for three different research methods to take place. The expected outcomes, as well as the risks.

When the lights in the room brightened, I'd lost about a third of who I'd invited. It was close to my calculations. I was disappointed, of course. I'd wanted them all to see the brilliance of the research design, but some of my friends were purists in ethics. I found them hypocrites, of course. They'd accepted Masters and Johnson's research on the Human Sexual Response. Research funded by Playboy icon Hugh Heffner who reportedly sexually abused women who worked for him—but my friends had to do what they had to do, and so did I.

Back at our bunker, our team began our work in earnest. First, we decided how to design future females to fight against unwanted sexual intercourse and unwanted pregnancies if, somehow, they did occur. We studied natural defenses of animals and insects. Insects presented us with the most promising findings, particularly bombardier beetles.

"This beetle uses explosive secretions called benzoquinones to destroy its enemies when attacked," I explained to the group. "If we can cut the genome that permits the development of this amazing feature in bombardier beetles and place it into a mammal's sexual organs—say a mouse or a monkey—targeting the Bartholin glands, vagina, or the uterus—would it have the same effect?"

Serjey, a neurobiologist, said thoughtfully, "With epigenome editing, it could be possible. It would need to be triggered with proper neurological responses from the brain. That would be tricky to achieve. And the chemical is toxic. The female would need to generate it and be immune to it."

His partner Raja nodded in agreement and added, "To trigger it, you'd have to be sure to elicit the female's fear, anger, or sense of threat at the exact moment of sexual intercourse to test if you were successful. That would be—difficult."

I saw that the idea made some researchers uncomfortable, not so much because of the thought of the animal studies but where the studies would lead after that.

"Let's begin with mice," I suggested. "At the moment of intercourse, we'll elicit a loud noise, and perhaps a startle response will give us the time we need to see if there is a reaction."

We removed the genome segments from the beetles and placed them into the mice where we wanted them as their embryos developed. At breeding age, we tested them with conflicting results. The females burned every single one of the male mouse genitalia. Not only that, but the males died less than an hour later. Unfortunately, so did the females. We determined for the males that it was related to the caustic agent that burned into blood vessels, causing exsanguination. For the females, it was the same. They should have been immune, but something kept them from being protected from themselves. Maybe it was the species, or perhaps the genome wasn't cut or placed precisely. Though it was only partially successful, I decided to move on.

"Monkeys next," I ordered. The crates arrived in four days with twelve male and twelve female rhesus specimens. With this group, I decided to divide them into six mating pairs that would give us embryos and six that would serve as a vaccine test subject group—three females to receive the vaccine and three males to be our additional test subjects later.

Jade visited me in the lab from time to time, her

growing belly a poignant reminder of why I was doing this, although I hated animal research. And I hated myself when I saw her face as she gazed at the monkeys, clearly repulsed at what I was doing.

"El, monkeys? Really? Do you have to? It's cruel. It's not worth it. *I'm* not worth it. They didn't choose this!"

"What did you think was going to happen here, Jade? That we'd just start editing humans, and everything would be perfect? It doesn't work that way. We must be sure the process works, that the sections we are removing from the beetle and inserting into a mammal do what we want them to do. Don't be so...so..." I was going to say "ignorant," but the word hung there in my throat. It didn't make any difference. She knew what I was going to say, and it hurt just as much as if I'd said it.

She ran out crying. I wanted to chase her, to hold her, and tell her it was going to be okay. That I was an ass. That this was a sacrifice we all had to make, even them, to save so many more. I wish I had. Maybe things would have been different.

We worked in our labs crafting our CRISPR-CAS9 GEO for delivery into our test subjects targeting the vaginal tissue, the Bartholin glands, and the uteruses of the females. During this time, we let the rhesus males and females socialize. We monitored the female fertility cycles. When we were ready, we injected the virus with the bombardier genome into the females at the very end of their cycle and waited until their next cycle came along. It was about twenty-seven days. Because the rhesus mate quickly and frequently, we elected to use electrified floor panels to stimulate our negative response. As soon as the males mounted the females, we'd press a button to deliver a shock. Nothing happened except we had angry and upset monkeys, who later resumed trying to mate after we paused to determine whether there was a desired result or not. We quickly separated them and went back to the drawing board.

Jade was now twenty-five weeks pregnant. We knew the baby was a girl, and we were relieved. It would be easier to have a girl. We could modify her genes as well, once we knew it was safe.

"What shall we call her?" I asked Jade, knowing she probably had the perfect name picked out.

"I'm thinking Kali," Jade said. "A form of the Mother Goddess—the protector. Mistress of death, time, and change. What better name for a little girl who will bring change to a brand-new world?"

I kissed Jade's lips, losing myself in their soft sweetness, inhaling her amber perfume. Pregnancy made her even softer, sweeter all over as if she had become the Mother Goddess herself, passing on the legacy to the child within her. "Kali she is, then," I said. A slight chill rippled down my spine as I confirmed the baby's name.

The pager on my belt buzzed. I raced to the lab and halted as I faced the horror that the rest of the team was witnessing. The female monkeys in the glass observation room were screaming, their flesh bubbling, somehow liquefying from the inside out. Their tissue plopped on the floor as they writhed in agony. They fell, their mouths open wide, gasping like fish suffocating.

"Euthanize them," I said. "Pinpoint where we went wrong. Incinerate the bodies. Order more, ASAP." I spun around and walked out. I'm sure I sounded like an automaton. Cold. Callous. Truth was, I was shaking, nauseated by guilt. I couldn't bear what I'd just witnessed. What I'd just caused. If I'd broken down in front of everyone, they would have all quit on the spot. I knew it in my heart. I couldn't allow that—not with so much at stake.

The male monkeys in the glass chamber next door had seen, heard, everything. What effect did it have on them? I wasn't an animal behavioralist. Didn't we have one on the team? We had a veterinarian. At the time, I thought that was good enough.

Jade was inconsolable when I told her about the

delayed results on the females and their deaths. We were in our quarters, which looked more like a prison pod but with a double-sized platform bed rather than bunks. We sat on stools attached to a round stainless steel table.

"That's so horrible, El! And you just let it happen?"

"I stopped it soon as I could. Their suffering served no purpose at that point."

Jade's entire body pulled away from me, although she was still sitting on a stool. She repeated, "Served no purpose?"

I sighed. "Yes. If continuing to watch them die told us more about our genome placement, if we needed more information, we, or I would have to let it continue."

She seemed to be reeling from this information. Not knowing exactly how to handle this part of *me*, the researcher. Then she said, "Do you think, maybe, that the genome placement isn't enough? That you need an emotional transmitter? What if you linked some kind of..."

I interrupted her, though I knew I shouldn't have, but she didn't have the experience that I had. "That's not possible, Jade. We don't have that capability."

"But..."

I got up and stepped over to kiss her. "You have a great day. I love you. Never forget it." I felt her eyes on me as I walked away. I wish I'd listened to her more closely.

Before the new female monkeys arrived, our team was careful to be precise about the genome extraction from the bombardier beetles and the vaccine development, having examined our previous mistake. When they came, it took us a few weeks to prepare them. We gave the vaccine at the proper interval, making sure we socialized the monkeys beforehand. I wondered if I should have ordered additional male monkeys as well. What if the current male monkeys who watched the other females die had decreased desire to mate with the new female monkeys when it was time? The veterinarian assured me this would not be the case. Even if there was some sort of perceived risk in being with the females, it might make them more attractive to the males. Apparently, rhesus monkeys were, according to 2013 research, known to have an attraction to elements of risk-taking in their make-up. I hoped he was right.

While we waited for the females to hit their fertility cycle, I worked with the team on the other three female monkeys and their embryos, now that they were pregnant. We studied the epigenetic factor we considered for insertion into the embryos and alternatives that included more than just genomes from the bombardier beetle.

Jade busied herself talking to team members. I liked that she spent time in the lab learning about the project, although I saw how troubled she was by the animal research. She spent a lot of time with our engineers who oversaw nanotechnology, which included pico-technology and elements of artificial intelligence or AI, which I found curious, but she always liked learning about machines and so on. If she didn't get in their way or cause difficulties, then she was welcome. Her therapeutic presence helped many of them, and I saw some of them sitting down to talk with her in what were likely unofficial therapy sessions, which were undoubtedly very good for them as well.

"The females were vaccinated last night," I told her at breakfast. "If all goes well, it won't be a pretty sight. The males will be severely injured and likely die later. All of them will suffer under the intermittent electrical shocks during mating."

Her lower lip trembled. "I should be there. They are suffering for Kali. They don't know it, but they are."

I wondered that her psychologist brain could rationalize that being there would somehow be honorable. "It's really best you aren't there, Jade. You got so upset last time. Best you stay here, okay? I'll come back soon as it's over and tell you about it."

She saw my face and understood there was no use

arguing. She hugged me as best she could with that thirty-week belly bump between us, then I headed to the lab.

The dividing doors between each female and male monkey pair opened, and our observers were poised, fingers over the buttons, ready to deliver electrical currents to the pairs when mating began. Nothing happened at first. The monkeys sat quietly beside each other. Then mounting happened and quickly. Team members barely had time to push the buttons. As soon as they did, the males were off again and electrical currents were delivered to monkeys who were already separated, making for three pairs of angry non-mating monkeys.

"You have to have precise timing," I said. "This is a very quick mating sequence. As soon as you see the males mount, you must wait half a second then deliver the shock, or it will be too late, understood?"

Everyone nodded. The next go round was almost successful but still ended up with angry monkeys and no positives. It took thirty minutes before they were calm again. "Let them mount a couple of times. Let them feel comfortable, and then do it." Three was a charm. When they hit the button at the right time, the male monkeys first yelled along with the females from the shock, and then bubbling of acid delivered from the female's genitals was apparent on the male genitals. The burning of their tissue commenced, and the males were in horrific pain. The females appeared unharmed.

One of the observers turned toward me. "Shall we put them down now, ma'am?"

"No," I responded. "We need to observe everything. Keep filming. Catalog it all from beginning to end. Observe the females as well."

The shock on his face was evident, but I didn't have time to explain. Today was very different from the last time. This was the experiment. This needed complete observation and documentation.

I returned to our quarters, excited to tell Jade about

today's success, but she was not there. I didn't think much of it, since I knew she'd taken to going to the indoor gym we'd created so our staff could stay physically fit. I changed into workout clothes, thinking I'd join her, maybe run three miles, and do a weight circuit or two, but when I entered the gym, she wasn't there. Now I was confused. It was past lunchtime and too early for dinner. We always ate together. Where could she be?

I stepped out of the gym, into the corridor, and nearly ran right into her as she came in. She looked at me wide-eyed, surprised.

"Hey," she said. "Done already?"

"Came to work out with you," I said. "Figured you'd be here. I was worried when you weren't. You okay?" I took in her color. She was a little flushed. Overall, she looked fine. I looked down. Was her belly bigger than usual?

"Never better." She smiled. "I got to talking with some of the engineers on my way here and kept walking with them down D corridor. I was just coming back."

I looked over that way. D corridor was our nano- and pico-tech department. *I should kick myself,* I thought. I knew Jade liked to socialize, and why would I worry if she spent some time talking with others? Certainly, she found their work interesting. I smiled back, trying to let it all go. "Great," I said. "Let's walk a couple miles on the treadmill. Maybe turn on something mindless while we work out? *Big Bang?*"

"Sure." She made her way to a machine, and we started them up.

It was about an hour before I was supposed to get up for work, four-thirty, when Jade whispered in my ear.

"Can't sleep. Going for a walk. I love you." She kissed my cheek.

"Love you," I mumbled, rolled over, and went back to sleep. She'd done this before a few times whenever insomnia hit her, and she always came back ready to snuggle and snooze. When my alarm went off, her side of the bed was empty. She wasn't in the dining facility for breakfast, and there was no time to track her down. I had to go through more test results from yesterday and consider the next steps toward human trials.

It was just after noon when two engineers came to speak with me. "You need to come," one said. "It's urgent."

I tried to get them to explain, but they refused. When I demanded an explanation, they said it was about Jade. My stomach lurched. "What happened? Tell me."

"It's best if you come with us, Doctor," was all I could get out of them. I quickly left with them, angry and confused.

When I entered their lab, Jade was in a room behind glass panels, much like in my own research space. Not only that, but she was up on a table in stirrups, a sheet draped over her as if she were about to give birth. Someone was next to her in a surgical gown, a set of instruments beside them.

"What is the meaning of this?" I started in a low growl. "What the hell?" My voice grew louder.

A voice spoke over the intercom. "Dr. Foster, Director Sullivan here. They've all acted on my authority. Jade asked for this trial."

I walked to the glass, pressed my face and my hands against it, trying to meet Jade's gaze.

"Jade?"

Her eyes were on me, apologetic, reassuring, and something else—beyond description—almost transformative.

She opened her mouth. I read her lips. *I love you.*

A monitor in the room showed Jade's vital signs and the baby's heartbeat.

An engineer walked over to stand beside me. I recognized him. Dr. Leonard Hanover.

"What did you do to my wife, Leo?" I didn't bother to contain the anger in my voice. I kept my eyes on Jade.

Dr. Hanover sighed, clearly unhappy with his role of

having to explain what was happening to my wife. "Jade came to us requesting genomic modifications to her baby. Including nano-pico-tech and AI enhancement throughout the entire nervous system. We believed at first that you knew about this. Later, it became apparent that you did not."

He held a folder out to me. I only glanced at it as I took it from him, noting the white of his lab coat contrasting with his dark skin. Dr. Hanover continued. "When you open the folder, you'll see the full design. It is," he cleared his throat, "extensive. Jade went well beyond biologic self-defense and control of pregnancy. She understands that the human species is..."

"Doomed." I finished, suddenly aware now what Jade had been up to, my mind afraid to fully comprehend what she'd done. Jade and I often spoke about the concept of human extinction versus human evolution after reading Professor Stephen Hawking's book *Brief Answers to the Big Questions,* published in 2018 just after his death. "Not exactly correct, but I understand where you're going. What she was thinking..."

Jade was breathing rapidly now, her body shifting on the birthing table. I saw her mouth open as she breathed out and in. I wanted to be with her. Instead, I was helpless, only able to watch in horror and fascination as beads of sweat formed on her brow and ran down her face.

"Can't you let me in with her?" I called out, knowing Director Sullivan was watching. Listening.

"Impossible," the director responded. "Given the number of modifications, we can only allow the physician inside."

I heard Jade moaning through the glass now. Her body was shaking on the table. The physician kept trying to keep her calm, but Jade kept trying to get up. When the physician placed her hands on Jade to adjust the fetal heart monitor, Jade did the impossible. She sat up, grasped the woman around the torso, and threw her across the room into the far wall, knocking her unconscious.

I backed away from the glass in shock. Jade rose from the table and stood on the floor, her feet planted more than shoulder width apart. She squatted. Thousands of thin spidery fibers shot from her skin in silky iridescent threads. They attached themselves to the walls, the glass, the floor, and the ceiling, anchoring her to the surfaces around her. It was difficult to see her now—the fibers were so thick, like she was wrapped in a fine cocoon. When security attempted to enter the room to help the doctor, the door would not open.

"Jade!" I screamed her name over and over. Leo reached out and gripped my hand. I shook it off and went to the glass. I still couldn't see anything. "Jade!"

A voice over the intercom spoke. "Jade, it will be okay—just breathe..."

A strange tone emanated from the room, high pitched like a metallic whine, then like the white noise of radio static. There was a sound like a large gushing of water and then silence. None of us could see anything, then we heard a loud "plop." Seconds passed as security tried to get past the door, and then there was the cry of a baby—a fierce cry. Still unable to see, we heard the crew blast through the door, and along with the baby's cries, I heard, "Oh, my God...so much blood!"

It was Jade's wish that the staff bring Kali to me as soon as possible after her birth. One of Jade's absolute conditions. I think she knew she would not survive the birth, and the only way that I might bond with the baby was if I held her right away. I didn't want this bundle they brought to me now—this thing that killed my dearest wife. This was a monster, a thing of rape; this experiment gone horribly wrong. It should have been aborted. It had ripped my dearest Jade to pieces.

A Sister dressed in a black jacket, black shirt, and

pants—she wrapped an arm around me, though I tried to fight her off at first.

"Ellis," she said. "This child, Kali, is part of Jade. She wanted you to care for her, to help guide her. Jade trusted you to do this. Yes, this is hard. Jade knew it would be. She also knows that Kali is going to help save humankind. She will change our species so it can survive."

I looked at the Sister, into her dark eyes, my tears, my rage, my anger crashing in waves around me. I heard Jade's voice, felt Jade all around me, and I knew what this woman said was true. The Sister handed me an envelope. "This is for you, as well." Then she placed Kali into my arms.

The baby's skin was without a blemish. Her hair was golden brown and thick for a newborn. The eyes were wide and full of intelligence.

Holding Kali in the crook of one arm, I opened the envelope and pulled out a paper. It was a note, and in it a Greek silver coin with an owl embossed on it. I held the coin and read the note.

> *The Greek Goddess Athena, goddess of wisdom, was reputed to have an owl, but no one has ever known its name. I have always called it Mutatio---'change.' You will change the world, Jade. I know it.*
>
> *Love, Mama Ann.*

So, this was what my mother had given Jade that day. I gazed down at Kali.

"Well, we have your middle name."

A name selected in different ways by three women. A middle name that reflected her destiny. *Change.* I held her close and inhaled her scent. Maybe I imagined it, but she somehow smelled like Jade's amber perfume. My emotions surged. She was part of Jade, and so, a part of me.

I love you. I tentatively pressed a thought to her.

Kali began crying, and furiously. One of the medical engineers came forward. "She needs to eat now, Doctor."

I started to hand her back. The engineer smiled. "No. From you. Breast is best."

"But, I..."

They pulled up a chair, unbuttoned my shirt, and helped me unfasten my bra. I was confused. One of the Sisters showed me how to hold her.

"I don't have milk. I wasn't preg—," I protested, but then Kali quieted, her attention fixed on my breast. A metallic sheen glazed across her eyes. She opened her mouth. Spider-silk-thin tendrils emerged and found my nipple as I drew her close. There was a stinging sensation.

An engineer explained, "Kali's AI components will trigger your prolactin hormone for milk production. She will receive exactly what she needs for optimum health."

I stared into her eyes and thought I could feel her hunger, her gratitude, her joy. And yet, given her make-up I wondered if this child, this creature, would be considered an entirely new species. Did Jade manage, in some strange way, to abort mankind with her sacrificial birth?

Welcome to a brand-new day.

Was that my thought or hers?

TEN DAYS' GRACE

By Foz Meadows

Julia Kettan first knew her husband was dead when she looked out the window and saw a car emblazoned with the crest of the Bureau of Family Affairs pulling up in the driveway. Her legs went weak, though whether from relief or fear she couldn't tell. Robert hadn't come home the previous evening. She'd phoned it in that morning to both the police and the Bureau, not wanting to risk a second major infraction under the Spousal Laws in case anything really had happened, despite being convinced that Robert had just drunk too much after work and decided to sleep at a friend's. He'd done that before and, each time, she'd forced herself to let the Bureau know, just in case. And now, it had actually happened. Robert was gone, and a man in a suit was walking solemnly toward her door—she could see him through the kitchen window, pausing to straighten his tie, raising a hand for the buzzer—and it took all her strength not to burst out into terrified, sob-drenched laughter. *At least Lily's at school,* she told herself wildly. *At least she doesn't have to be here for this, the naked, ugly part of it all.* Fingers shaking, she finished programming the cleanser, and then the buzz came; it was time, it was time, and the questions were already on her lips—*how did it happen?* And *what comes next?*

The agent on the other side of the door was younger than he'd seemed through the glass—not much older than her own thirty-three years, which was some relief. The patriarchs were the ones to watch out for. Julia made herself take in his brown eyes, clean-shaven jaw, and black hair with impartiality, trying to let nothing show in her face. But of course, she was an open book to him; even as he opened his mouth, she could tell he knew that she knew why he'd come, and that he was unsurprised by her knowledge.

"Mrs. Julia May Kettan, formerly Julia Mai Liu?"

"Yes."

"I'm Agent Sora James with the Bureau of Family Affairs. May I come in?"

She waved him through. No smile, no grief. As blank as blank. "Of course."

They sat in the lounge room opposite one another. Agent James had a file under one arm, which he laid down on the coffee table before lacing his fingers together. Though clearly uncomfortable, he managed to meet her gaze.

"Mrs. Kettan, at seven-oh-five this morning, you alerted us as to the possible disappearance of your husband, Mr. Robert Anthony Kettan. It is my unfortunate duty to inform you that your suspicions were correct; Mr. Kettan was involved in a traffic collision at approximately eleven-fifty last night on the eastbound lane of Jury Road. His vehicle was clocked at almost double the speed limit; it seems likely that he was trying to reach home before curfew kicked in. From what we can gather, he lost control of the car at the Maven Street corner, skidded, and flipped. The accident was reported almost instantly by another motorist, but your husband was pronounced dead at the scene." He paused. "I'm sorry for your loss."

Julia nodded. A numb feeling had started to spread through her stomach and up her throat. She'd never loved Robert, but after twelve years together, he'd become the devil she knew. Now she'd have her pick of unfamiliar fiends. If you could call it a pick.

As Agent James reached for the file, she fixed her eyes on a distant corner of the room, unable to bear the innocuous tap of stylus on screen.

"You have one child—Lily Alicia Kettan, born July 8, 2048, now aged twelve years. Is that correct?"

Her voice seemed to come from far away. "It is."

"You have no exigency partner registered with the Bureau under Spousal Law 5.14?"

"No."

"And have you attempted to register any such person in the past two to fourteen days?"

"No."

Agent James sighed. There was a faint *click-click* as he entered her responses. *Routine,* Julia told herself. *That's what this is. A routine.*

"According to our records, Robert was not Lily's progenitor."

"No. He wasn't. Her father was already married." At Agent James's raised eyebrow, she shook her head and corrected herself. "I'm sorry. Her progenitor. Of course, Robert was her father."

"I see."

Falling pregnant with Lily had been her first infraction against the Spousal Laws. Like homosexuality and abortion, single parenthood had been illegal ever since the National Family Party came to power nearly three decades ago. As soon as the cause of Julia's sudden nausea was correctly diagnosed, she'd been brought before the Bureau and called to account for the genesis of her not-allowed-to-be-illegitimate offspring. The child's progenitor, she'd told them, was her employer, Roy Sovas, a kind man some twenty years her senior whose wife had produced a single sickly daughter and a string of miscarriages. Divorce was impossible. Something had to be done.

Armed with her testimony, the Bureau took a DNA sample from Roy and used it to prove paternity, although he, to his lasting credit, had already confessed to the affair. For his part in their joint violation of the Spousal Laws, Roy received a docked salary, a black mark on his citizenship record, and a formal reminder that he was forbidden from contacting either Julia or their child for the next eighteen years, until the zygote who was to become Lily had reached its majority. For her part, Julia was given a choice: either give birth and then surrender her newborn to an adoptive couple or take a husband. There was also the matter of finding a new job and a black mark similar to Roy's, but compared to the choice of abandoning her child or raising it with a man she didn't love, such trifles paled into insignificance.

In the end, she'd opted for marriage. She knew of no suitable candidates, but then, if she had done, the affair with Roy would hardly have been necessary. Fortunately, the Bureau was well-versed in human weakness, and kept a roster of available men—and women, should the need arise, although it much less frequently did—who were willing to marry such as her. That exercise, at least, contained some element of choice, albeit a meager one. Robert had seemed the lesser of several evils. They met twice, agreed to marry, and then it was done. Lily's existence was legitimized by this facade of wedded parentage. Love didn't enter into it, or competence, or care, or even genetics. Every child, the National Family Party said, should have both a father and mother, come what may. And as Lily was still years from her majority, the fact of Robert's death didn't matter either. Once again, the choice was Julia's— either give her daughter away or marry another man to ensure Lily's proximity to an official father figure.

She'd been silent for a long time, pretending this not-quite-conversation with Agent James was heading in a different direction. She looked at him, hoping she might somehow have slipped backward in time to an era when this sort of thing didn't happen, but still the stylus stabbed inexorably downward.

Tap. Tap.

"You understand," said Agent James, "that the Bureau's concern is only for Lily's well-being. A child raised by only one gender, no matter how lovingly, cannot ever be more than a half-being."

"I understand," croaked Julia, although she did not, could not, never had, never would, least of all now, when Robert, whose existence should have protected her from this eventuality, was gone, and how was she to feel about that, anyway?

"You do not have to decide just yet," said Agent James, so gently that Julia found herself hating him. "First, there is the funeral to attend to. Afterward, however—"

"Yes," she said bitterly, "I remember. Ten days' grace in which to find a husband."

"Ten days' grace," said Agent James, nodding his head. "Shall I bring you the list of candidates once things are sorted?"

Fuck your candidates, Julia wanted to scream at him.

"Yes," she said.

Telling Lily was hard, but not because of Robert. All the grief her daughter felt at his death was warped—subsumed, even—by fear of what came next. Who would this stranger be, this sudden unfamiliar man whose presence would be a daily reminder of what was lost, an intrusion into matters of which he could have no possible conception? Even at the level of words, something was being imposed and taken away. In memory, Robert would become a *caregiver*, and father no more—that title now belonged to a foreign successor, in law if not in Lily's heart. Julia held her girl close, putting one arm around those slender ribs, that sweet child-spine not yet straightened with the confidence of breasts nor hunched with the burden of them, and let the snot-sobs soak into her jumper. Lily knew whose biological offspring she was and wasn't—that honesty, at least, had been dealt with years ago—but for all that Robert had been far from Julia's ideal, he had at least cared for their daughter. *Their daughter*. Julia rolled the phrase through her brain and decided it was as accurate as any; or, if there were a more suitable naming, she couldn't think of it.

"Why can't it just be us?" Lily cried. "Why can't they leave us *alone*?"

Julia made no answer. She had seen her daughter's reports for the mandatory class called Civics and Virtue, even taken perverse pride in the quantity of glowing grades they earned. Lily knew why this was happening, but knowing why and feeling why were two different things. That was her current lesson.

By comparison, the funeral was easy. Closed casket—she'd asked Lily whether she wanted to see Robert again or not, a request which elicited yet more tears and a tightly shaken head—and a minimum of religion. Robert would have wanted more pomp. Like many who signed up to marry the unwed mothers, he'd been a true believer. But Julia had no stomach for priests and their moralism and forbade the single church official from saying anything more than the basic death-grace. Robert's male relatives kept their condolences to a minimum, all except Orson, his younger brother, whose clammy hands on hers proved as slippery and unwelcome as his effusive condolences, greasing her ears like so much wax.

As for the women—well. They were older. They remembered the Roaring Twenties and Shining Tens, years before Julia's predicament was ever etched into law. She was only a child when it happened, lacking the power to prevent the present day, but perhaps they might have changed things if they'd tried. *Perhaps, perhaps.* They patted her softly, and clucked, and looked away. Lily stood like a reed, fists clenched, and did not cry. Julia felt proud of her for that. Under the weight of so much pity, tears were to have been expected. But she had already cried, at length, in private. Such tender emotions were not for public display, and by law, in any case, these people were no longer her relatives.

Julia's mother had died of cancer before Lily's third birthday; her father was still alive, but in some ways attending would have been more painful for him than anyone. To be bricked in by the solid, living-and-breathing proof of what the law had done to his daughter—a thing that had grieved her mother enough in life, sapping comfort from those final years—would be unendurable. She had phoned him instead; they talked, though it was a conversation more composed of silences than speech, and that was enough for either of them.

As Julia hung up, she heard him weeping.

The wake passed in a blur. She moved through her house, touching what was hers, as though trying to draw strength from it, and watching as Robert's relatives took away those things that had belonged to him alone. Her new husband would not want them, she assumed; certainly, she did not. Throughout it all, she drew herself up and moved, clean-limbed and steady, like the most perfect clockwork woman ever built, like a computer simulation of herself, like a ghost whose feet did not quite touch the ground. And then, just as suddenly as it had filled, her house was empty again, the sudden absence of Robert's things balanced out by a newfound profusion of salad-bearing Tupperware containers, crockery smeared with pie-rind, plates covered with uneaten meat and a litter of plastic cups. Lily went upstairs to weep again in private, but it wasn't until Julia heard her daughter's door slam shut that she let herself drop, spraddle-kneed on the carpet, and cry with the silent experience of a mother who cannot—must not—be overheard.

Agent James returned the following day. Had she in any way wanted to see him, Julia might have called it a courtesy visit. He needn't have bothered; the candidate files were digital, after all. Her first instinct was to stop him at the threshold, but the habit of hospitality was too deeply ingrained to ignore. Instead, she invited him in and made tea, which they both drank, before stylus-clicking her way through the list of available men. Agent James sat opposite and watched her, silent as still water.

"There's a reason I've come in person," he said finally when she was done pretending to form meaningful opinions about a group of strangers.

"Oh?"

"A Mr. Orson Wallace Kettan has petitioned for consideration as your husband."

Julia felt her blood run cold. "*He* wants to marry me?"

"He was your husband's brother. That holds a lot of weight with the Bureau."

"Weight," echoed Julia.

Agent James closed his eyes, recalling words from memory. "When brothers live together and one of them dies and has no son, the wife of the deceased shall not be married outside the family to a strange man. Her husband's brother shall go in to her and take her to himself as wife and perform the duty of a husband's brother to her." His eyes snapped open, brown as wet earth. "Deuteronomy 25:5. A favorite verse, for some. I am instructed to inform you that, should none of our candidates rouse in you any strong preference, Mr. Orson Kettan would be looked on as a more than favorable alternative. In point of fact, were you desirous of removing the black mark from your citizenship record—and, by extension, from Lily's—such a match would, I'm told, hold great sway with our records division."

For a long moment, Julia stared at Agent James, sifting through the balance of his words, looking for some sign or other that the sarcasm she would swear to having heard was genuine, and not just a product of her own shock. Sure enough, one corner of his mouth was twisted upward like the tail of an italicized serif. Julia sucked in breath.

"And why the fuck should I care about your records division?"

Agent James grinned. "You shouldn't. I certainly don't." One hand reached inside his jacket. "Mind if I smoke?"

"Please," said Julia, too startled by her own boldness and the reaction it had generated to form the usual protests. She watched as Agent James withdrew a polished cigarette case and a matching silver lighter from his pocket. He set these accoutrements down beside the file as though they were not completely incongruous in the context—or anachronistic, even, especially the case, from which he extracted not one, but two slim cigarettes, wrapped in white and gold paper. Julia had never smoked before in her life, but now she took the proffered tobacco in hand, pressing one end softly to her lips as the lighter sparked up. She inhaled, watching as the fire took, and felt her lungs seize with smoke. She coughed and coughed, which Agent James ignored. He lit his own cigarette and sucked on it, the slender cylinder strangely effeminate between his long, square-nailed fingers.

There was no ashtray, and Julia felt too rooted to the spot to fetch one. Instead, she tapped the gray leavings of this unfamiliar vice onto the tabletop, a sign for her guest to do likewise.

"What do you want?" she whispered.

By way of answer, Agent James tossed her the lighter. Julia barely managed to catch it without dropping her cigarette. Confused, she looked to him for an explanation, but none was forthcoming. She stroked the lighter with her thumb. It was filigreed rather than flat, embossed with subtle designs. Daring another suck of tobacco—it burned her throat and lungs, but the motion was soothing—she held up the object and stared at it, looking for clues.

She didn't have to look hard. Though some of the detail had been worn away with use, the filigreed images were still visible: a series of pairs of naked men, twined and grasping as they fucked one another. Not contraband all by itself, but if the vice pages could be believed, people had been arrested for less, or for as much. Julia shoved the lighter back on the table and stared at the man across from her. Agent Sora James of the Bureau of Family Affairs had as good as admitted to the crime of being homosexual.

"There are more of us than you'd think," he said softly,

taking another long breath of his cigarette. "In government, that is. Even the Bureau admits its working hours are inimical to the maintenance of a healthy family life. Of course, they'll still refuse promotion past a certain point if you don't exhibit your normalcy through wedded bliss, the idea being that, above a certain salary range, the problem takes care of itself. But we're still there. Don't ask; don't tell."

He looked at her, long and steady. "I hate the logic of what we do. I want to change it. But so long as I'm single, they'll never let me near enough the law to matter."

It wasn't quite a proposal. Even so, the question hung in the air.

"Why me?" asked Julia.

"You have a black mark on your file," said Agent Sora James. "You've disobeyed before. And you're not a believer. That might make you less...inimical...to someone like me. You have a daughter, which works out for both of us. Fatherhood is valuable. And having met you, I don't believe you want to choose between that—" He stabbed his cigarette toward the file, "—and the devout brother Orson. Consider me a third alternative."

If one argument in particular could be said to have blighted Julia and Robert's relationship, it was his constant desire to impregnate her with a child of his own blood—to be progenitor and father, both. Julia had never said as much, but her suspicion had always been that, had she acquiesced, Lily would not have received nearly half so much love from Robert as she had done. Why waste energy on a child that wasn't his, whose status was already tainted by her mother's decision to sleep with a married man? Robert had argued with her—pleaded, even—but though she bent toward him in all other ways, on this one thing Julia had remained firm, had been *able* to remain firm, as the law had not yet stripped the rights of married women to access birth control, though the issue remained a contentious one. She would not produce a child that further tied her to a man she didn't love when their marriage had only ever been a legal convenience. But there had still been sex—awkward at first, then more a matter of habit, but always unpleasant when compared to her memories of Lily's conception.

"You have...lovers?" She faltered on the question, unsure of the right terminology.

"Yes," said Sora James, who had suddenly stopped being Agent in her thoughts. "I take *lovers*. My interests do not run to women, and never have. On that count, I will not bother you."

"Could I—" She stopped, unable to get the question out. How did one ask permission for infidelity? Still, he grinned, despite her hesitance.

"You may."

A great rush of breath escaped her. Julia stared at the cigarette in her hand, which was mostly ash by now, and let it fall on the table. There were worse alternatives, and within her allotted ten days' grace, the notion of finding a more meaningful offer was absurd. At least she'd met this man; at least he, too, was taking a risk. She picked up the lighter from where it had sat on the table, forced herself to contemplate its images anew. Then, she gripped it, brief and tight, and threw the silver box to Sora, who caught it skillfully.

"Call it in," she said.

TOGETHER, TOUCHING

By Tenea D. Johnson

Here we were again, together, bruised not broken
—more sisters than blood could make us.

Covered in it, because she had chosen a way that they'd
barred us from, the ones with means and
money enough to go somewhere safe to undo what they'd
done as well as what had been done to them.

There she went, through the swinging doors where I
couldn't follow.
I'd called the paramedics. She needed help.
And this time I couldn't be that.

If she didn't die, neither would I, I told myself when they
sentenced me,
closed the cage, took away my name,
though she would never forget. And never let me.

Prisoners cannot write one another.
So every Sunday I sought communion, seeking her in the
pews, the only place they let us rest, thinking we'd mistake it for deliverance.

They'd moved her to another facility.
They won't call it prison, just as they won't admit they ran
out of room.
As if you couldn't tell by the bunks crowded in, the
faraway gazes, the fevered whispers.

All those years, apart.
Not one word between us.
We grieved alone, for everything.

But.
All those years, it held.
Then.

Overcrowding pushed us out early, toward each other.

By bond and bind, we were tied.

So, again we sat next to each other, touching,
as we hadn't since we became old women in young
bodies—
no space for secrets, only silence
that she broke.

*You don't know what's in you until something slices you
open and reaches in.*

When she said that,
I feared the years had twisted her,
toward them, and
away from reason, and me.

It was you I found, she said.

Doubt disappeared.

Hollow or whole,
even if I was alone,
it'd be her name on my lips
when I admitted
how it felt to see the last light leave,
how lucky I was to have found the ease of her,
when force-fed lies of family.

TINY TEETH

By Sarah Hans

I risk walking to the doctor's office from my workplace
because it's only a few blocks, and I think the fresh air will
do me some good. I don't tell anyone I'm going alone, or
that I'm walking. I know what they'll say. Outside, without an escort, without the safety of an enclosed vehicle,
my heart thrums like a tap dancer's quick steps. I should
be scared or thrilled by the prospect of imminent danger,
but I'm too frightened of the news waiting for me at the
doctor's office to be worried about much else. As I walk, I
become more and more convinced the news reports about
the gangs of feral children, with their pictures of mutilated
bodies and wide-eyed reporters speaking in quavering
voices, are attempts to manipulate us with fear. To keep
us inside. My coworkers are fools to walk in groups, to
rush from their cars to the office with Tasers and pistols
clutched in their fists. There is no danger here.

But then I see the girl, and I know I've made a mistake.
She crouches behind a bush, and when I spot her, I freeze
like a rabbit. She locks eyes with me and rises out of the
greenery. She's maybe four years old, though that's a guess.
It can be hard to tell the age of a child who has been feral
a long time, and I've never been around many children to
begin with, even before the virus made them violent.

She wears a tiny pair of denim shorts and a purple
T-shirt decorated with glitter hearts, both caked with gore.
Her hair was once styled in pigtails, but one side droops
sadly, and the other side is a crusted mass of red-brown

scab in place of hair. Her face is twisted into a permanent snarl. Her front two teeth are missing, which would make the expression she wears comical if she didn't have her hands held at the ready, fingers extended to grab, filthy fingernails ready to claw. A growl issues from low in her throat. Her eyes—bright green, shimmering like beetle wings in the sunlight—are filled with hatred and bloodlust. She smells like stale urine and blood and roadkill.

I fumble the pepper spray from my pocket as she lurches toward me. I hold down the trigger and close my eyes, flinching away from the stream. I remember the instructions: always aim, always look where you're pointing your weapon. But I can't look. I make a sound, a sort of squeal, the sound of a trapped herbivore facing a predator.

When I open my eyes, the girl is gone. Eyes squinted tightly shut and breath held against the burning cloud of pepper spray, I run the rest of the way to the doctor's office.

Dr. Heiss steeples his hands on the desk. Behind him, the nurse flashes me a tight, sympathetic smile. I know what he's going to say before he says it.

"Congratulations, Hailey. You're going to be a mother." He delivers the news as if it's a pizza—factually, without inflection, without excitement or dread. But at least he has the good sense not to smile.

The tight knot in my stomach unfurls, and bile rises in my throat. The nurse, who isn't much older than I am, brings me water in a paper cup. I gulp it down, my swallows very loud in the quiet room. "How do I get an abortion?"

The nurse stiffens and moves away from me. Dr. Heiss frowns. "Legally, in this state, I'm not allowed to discuss the option. We can make an appointment for you with the gynecologist next door. You'll like her a lot. She can guide you through the pregnancy."

My heart hammers, and the edges of my vision become ragged. I think of the girl with one pigtail, her depraved expression flashing in my mind, and a shudder ripples through me. "That's it? You're handing me a death sentence, just like that?"

He exchanges a look with the nurse, sighs, and leans back in his chair, letting his hands go to the armrests. "It's not a death sentence."

I crush the paper cup in my fist and throw it at him as I rise. "Fifty percent chance, Dr. Heiss. Fifty percent chance. I've been your patient for ten years, and that's the best you can offer me?"

"I'm sorry," he sighs, "but you knew the risks."

I pace the waiting room and bite my nails down to ragged nubs. I feel like I'm going to crawl out of my own skin, so I have to move. I don't want to risk going outside alone, not with the girl maybe out there, but the waiting room feels like a jail cell.

There's a woman sitting there with her kid on a leash, and I can't stop staring at them both. The woman is gaunt, hollow-eyed, and her son—it's hard to tell a kid's gender through the muzzle, but the T-shirt with a cartoon backhoe is probably a good indication he's a boy—sits on the floor trying to rip off the oven mitts taped over his hands. Going by his height, he's maybe three years old. He growls every time someone enters the office, and every time I pace past him. Everyone else in the waiting room sits on the far side, as far away from him as they can get, staring at their phones, pretending he isn't the most grotesquely fascinating thing in the room.

My phone dings when I receive the text from Tyler: *I'm here.* I move for the door, and the boy snarls and lunges at me, spittle flying. He brushes me with an oven mitt before his mother yanks his leash. I step out the door into the fresh air.

I slide into the passenger seat of Tyler's sedan. "What's going on, Hail?" His eyes are intense, frantic. He's guessed why I went to the doctor.

"I'm pregnant."

"We used protection."

"Urine tests don't lie."

"Did you sleep with anyone else?" His voice takes on an edge of panic.

I'm too numb to even be upset he's asking me that. "No, of course not."

"I just don't understand how this could happen."

"No birth control is one hundred percent safe," I hear myself saying, echoing Dr. Heiss. "Abstinence is the only way to be sure."

"Okay, so, how do we get rid of it?"

Seagulls wheel and shriek over the parking lot, looking for dropped tidbits. A couple approach the door to the doctor's office, and the gulls flap away. The man is pushing a stroller. The toddler strapped inside, wearing a pink dress and a muzzle decorated with shiny plastic jewels, screams like a banshee. The sound makes it impossible to think. Her open mouth is pink and red, and her teeth are like white needles snapping at the air. Her father walks robotically to the door, but her mother, for just an instant, meets my gaze through the windshield. In her eyes, I see regret and exhaustion and bone-deep sorrow. She turns and goes into the office, and the door shuts behind them, thankfully cutting off the screams.

"Can we just go home?" I ask.

"Can you give me a second to process this?" Tyler answers.

I sigh. "Abortions are illegal now." Nobody would have children anymore if they weren't.

"There has to be a way." His hands grip the steering wheel hard, as if he's imagining strangling his problems away.

"Of course there's a way. But I can't exactly Google it." My pregnancy is on record now. If something happens to the fetus, I have to be able to document a miscarriage, or I'll face jail time. It's pretty much my worst nightmare. I want to scream at Tyler that this is his fault because I want someone to blame, and if we sit here much longer, I'm going to do it. Tears sting my eyes. "Can we please go home? We have some time to figure this out."

"How long do we have?"

I press one hand against my abdomen. It doesn't feel

any different yet. How is it possible there's a tiny monster in there waiting to rip its way out of me? It doesn't seem real. "Dr. Heiss said they can't test for the virus until the second trimester. I'm about a month along. So we have about two months to figure it out. Obviously, I want this thing out of me sooner rather than later, but it doesn't have to be right this second." I do want it out right this second, but I need time to calm down, think, strategize. I can't just tell him to drive to the grocery store and buy me a gallon of bleach to drink.

But damn, I want to.

My friend Anna knows a woman. For a fee, she'll make a concoction. "It's one hundred percent safe," Anna tells me. "Legally speaking anyway. It's all natural too."

"What'll it do to me?"

She shrugs. "Nothing that fetus isn't going to do to you if you let it get any bigger."

Anna goes with me. I want Tyler to see this through with me, but I know better than to ask him. He already won't look at me, his eyes sliding away from mine, as if repelled by a magnet. I'm losing him. I need this thing out of me and over with as quickly as possible so we can get back to our lives.

The woman's house is on Fourth Street, in the dangerous part of town, a place I don't often go. I glance anxiously at each shadow, jumping every time a bush rustles, but I take comfort from Anna's confidence. She saunters up to the front door like she's done this a lot, which she probably has. She's always been the risk-taker in our friendship. I'm the boring one who stays at home and watches movies in my pajamas while Anna's out clubbing. Not for the first time, I'm thankful for her resourcefulness, her bravery, and the path she's blazed ahead of me. The gratitude almost chokes out the fear.

Almost. Down the street, under a streetlamp, there's a silhouette of a small person, a small person with one pigtail and her hands held up, ready to rip and tear. She's too far away for me to hear her, but I can almost feel the thrumming of her growl in my bones.

When the woman answers the door, Anna has to speak because I'm temporarily paralyzed. "Hey, Dee."

Dee is short—shorter even than I am—with white hair and a nose too big for her face. She narrows her rheumy eyes at us but nods understanding and opens the door, beckoning us in with a casual gesture. I glance back at the streetlamp, and when I'm sure the silhouette is no longer there, I follow Anna into the house. It smells like herbs— every herb except weed, ironically—and cat piss. There are four cats I can see, and I suspect there are more hiding. My nose immediately starts to itch. I stay close on Anna's heels, my heart thundering.

We go into the kitchen. Filthy dishes are piled on every surface, and crushed cockroaches cover the floor. There's a litterbox next to the oven, heaped with stinking piles of cat shit. Something foul-smelling simmers on the stove.

"You want the usual?" Dee opens the refrigerator.

"Yep." Anna places her hand on my arm.

"One hundred."

I fish the bills from my pocket and offer them. Dee snatches them from my hand and draws a bottle from the fridge door, slapping it into my palm. I cradle the bottle in my hands, staring at it. My salvation is a gray-brown sludge in an old coke bottle with a piece of cork shoved into the opening.

"Should I drink it now?" I ask.

Dee snorts. "Take it home. Get sick in your own bathroom."

"Is there anything else I should know before I drink it?"

"Drink it all if you want it to work."

So I do. Sitting at my kitchen table, dressed in the old clothes I usually reserve for painting parties and moving day, I drink the contents of the bottle. It has the texture of the sludge they give you for colonoscopy prep and tastes like stale beer. I have to alternate between gulps of abortion potion and soda just to get it all down.

Anna squeezes my hand. "I have to go to work. Just

remember, you're going to be okay."

Later, as I'm sobbing on the bathroom floor through the worst pain of my life, I hate her for saying that. I'm pretty sure nothing will ever be okay again.

I visit Dr. Heiss early one morning before work a week later. He frowns at my lab results on the computer monitor. "How do you know you had a miscarriage?"

I try to crane my neck to see the computer screen, but it's angled away from me. "There was a lot of cramping and blood. Isn't that what happens during a miscarriage?"

He nods. "Traditionally. But it appears you're still pregnant."

My stomach drops. "Could that be, like, residual hormones or something?"

"Afraid not." His eyes are very cold and blue when he looks at me again. "I'm not going to report you this time, Hailey, because your baby lived, but don't try this again."

I swear my heart skips a beat. "What?"

"I know parenthood is scary right now. But a cure for the virus will be found. It's not fair to murder an innocent child because you're scared of what motherhood will be like." He rises and removes his glasses, casually sliding them into the pocket of his coat. As he strides from the room, his parting shot is, "Don't be so selfish."

I bite back the scream that rises in my throat. *Selfish?* He thinks I'm selfish. Selfish because a fifty-fifty chance I'll survive the birth isn't good enough odds for me. Because I don't want to be like the hollow-eyed ghost people with their snarling, muzzled monsters on leashes, living day by day because humanity's last best hope is for a cure that might never come. I'm selfish, but he's the one forcing me to live this nightmare for what? His moral superiority?

I dress myself with shaking fingers, remembering the vomiting, the blood, the cramping, two days of pain and misery and shitting myself, two days of dying from poison, then another week of missed work while I recovered myself, and this parasite is still clinging to life inside me.

Rage makes my face hot. I have no idea what to do next. I think about wire coat hangers. I think about throwing myself in front of a car. If I miss any more work, I'll lose my job. I'm already losing Tyler.

The door opens, and I jump. It's the nurse. At first, I think she has my checkout papers, but instead she moves to me urgently and presses a postcard into my hand. "What's this?" I ask.

"Don't tell anyone where you got this," she hisses, curling her fingers around mine and giving them a firm squeeze. She nods once, her expression intense, and then hurries from the room like a phantom.

The postcard is glossy and shows a small yacht festooned with lights. *Visit the Ophelia,* it advertises. *Contact us now for harbor tours, day or night! Perfect for your next ladies' night out.* There's a phone number at the bottom.

I call outside the doctor's office on the sidewalk. I should wait, or maybe call from a pay phone, but I'm frantic, impatient. While the phone rings, a car pulls into the parking space in front of me. The man driving the car has the empty look all parents have, so I'm not surprised to see the car seat in the back. I register the oddness that the creature strapped into it isn't wearing a muzzle. I drop my phone in shock when the father steps from the car.

His arms and neck are covered in bruises and fresh scabs in the telltale half-moon shape of bites from a small, human mouth.

The screen on my phone is cracked, so I have to call the *Ophelia* from the phone at work after I clock in. A smooth voice answers. "Thank you for calling the *Ophelia*. This is Kendra."

"Kendra. I...a nurse gave me a card with...your number..."

"Are you pregnant, and you don't want to be?"

I'm not sure how to answer. All the air gusts from my lungs.

"I'll take that as a yes. What we do is completely legal and absolutely safe. Can you come in tonight?"

"Tonight?"

"That's our soonest opening. Do you have doubts about whether to go through with the procedure?"

Reality snaps back into place. "I just wasn't expecting it to be so soon."

"We want to help you get back to your life."

"How is it legal?"

"Our doctors wait to perform the procedure until we're in international waters." Kendra sounds impatient, like she's answered these questions so many times she has the script memorized. Before I can ask anything else, she says, "You'll experience a little spotting and possibly a small amount of cramping, but it should be minimal."

I suck in a shaking breath, my hand going to my sore belly. "How much will it cost?"

"Whatever you can afford. It's a sliding scale, thanks to our donors."

"You have donors?"

"People who want to ensure women maintain their reproductive rights in these troubled times."

A sense of relief washes over me. There are people who want to help.

My shift lasts until 7, so we set the meeting for 9 o'clock in the evening. I spend the rest of the day in an excited, terrified haze, getting little work done. When I get home in the evening, I tell Tyler the good news. He scowls.

"I might be cramping again, so someone should probably drive me," I say. "Anna will be at work, so I'd appreciate it if you could do it."

He won't look at me as he shakes his head. "I can't do that, Hail. That'll make me an accessory to murder."

"What?" I reel back from him. "Ty, I need you right now."

He still won't meet my eyes as he fidgets with the cords on his hoodie. "It's illegal. We could be prosecuted."

"I told you, they do the procedure in international waters. It's completely legal. And besides, what's the alternative?

Do you want me to die?"

"It's not for sure that you'd die."

I take two more steps back from him, my pulse thundering in my ears. "I thought you wanted me to get rid of it. Do you want me to carry it to term?"

He shrugs, pouting. I used to think that pout was cute, but right now, it's making me hate him in a way I've never hated anyone. "I don't know. Maybe. I've been thinking about it a lot this week. I just wish you'd let me help you make the decision. It's our baby, Hail."

"It's not a baby; it's a *monster*."

"It's a little bit of you and a little bit of me—"

"And a whole lot of virus!"

"—and you just want to kill it."

"It's going to chew its way out of me in the third trimester, Ty."

"They have medication for that now, tranquilizers and stuff."

"And what then? Say I do survive. Now we have a monster child." I'm shouting, images of the girl with one pigtail swimming in my vision. She's strapped into a car seat behind me as I drive around town, running errands, hollow-eyed and miserable—a slave to a creature I never wanted to create. I'm so angry, it's amazing my head hasn't popped off my body.

"Only until they find a cure." Tyler gives me his biggest, saddest puppy dog eyes, but it only sends a spike of fury through me.

"Oh my God, you're delusional." I'm so loud the neighbors are probably going to call the cops. "There isn't going to be a cure, Ty. It's been five years. This is it. Humanity is over. And we can live out the rest of our days together, happy, or we can live them out trying not to be eaten alive by the monster we made."

"But it's *our* monster. We made it. It's a sin to kill it."

"You don't even believe in God!" I grab my jacket and purse from the hallway and head for the door. I need to get out of here. Forever.

"We created it, and we should take responsibility for it," he calls after me.

"That's exactly what I'm doing," I retort. His keys are in the bowl by the door, and I grab them on my way out. I hope Anna will be okay with me sleeping on her sofa, and maybe also picking up my stuff later, because there's no way I'm ever coming back to Tyler. I never want to see him again, and I can't get his DNA out of me fast enough.

It's been more than a year since I wrecked my car and stopped driving, but I remember how to do it. I can't bring up GPS directions on my cracked phone, but I know the city pretty well, even at night. A driving instructor once told me never to hold in my tears while driving because they'll blur my vision, so I let them flow as I maneuver my way through the city toward the harbor. I must look a hot, sobbing mess to anyone who glances my way at a traffic light, but it's not like there are many drivers out after dark to see me, anyway. I try not to think about Tyler, I really do, but it's like my heart hurts so much, my brain doesn't even have a say over my body anymore.

I'm not far from the harbor, just after making a U-turn in a parking lot because I'm pretty sure I turned the wrong way, when flashing red and blue lights appear behind the car. I didn't do anything illegal. Did Tyler let his plates expire? My rage toward him flares anew. Automatically, my foot lifts from the accelerator and the wheel turns to the right, toward the curb.

Then I realize with a sinking feeling that Tyler must have called the cops and reported his car stolen. And he may also have told them where I was headed, what I was going to do. If I get pulled over, there's a really good chance they'll arrest me. And if I get arrested, who knows how long they'll keep me. I've read of women being handcuffed to hospital beds until their infected babies were born because they'd tried to end their pregnancies. It was for the safety of the unborn fetus. To these people, I'm now nothing but a glorified incubator.

Sucking in a breath, I mash the accelerator, twist the wheel to the left, and head for the freeway. Anna once ran from the cops with me in the car. She did it by getting on the freeway, driving like a lunatic, and getting off on the next exit, where she pulled into a parking lot and turned off the lights until our pursuers had passed. It was the most terrifying twenty minutes of my entire life until I found out I was pregnant. I'm not keen to reproduce the experience, but I also can't think of anything else to do.

The police car's sirens blare to life, and my heart clenches tight in my chest. A disembodied voice shouts, "Pull over." Now, in addition to car theft and murder, I can add fleeing the police to my rap sheet. My head spins, and I ignore a red light to turn onto the freeway ramp, dodging two SUV's.

I swerve between cars, speeding more than I ever have before, but I'm not Anna in the end. I flinch at every honked horn and screech of tires. I'm not fearless enough to drive at a speed that will shake the cops. I take an exit ramp, tear through a mall parking lot, and head again for the harbor. The police car pursues me doggedly. Panic claws its way up my throat, and I find myself cussing and shouting and slapping the steering wheel in frustration.

"PULL THE CAR OVER AND GET OUT WITH YOUR HANDS UP."

I direct my car east toward the harbor and run three red lights, somehow miraculously avoiding an accident on the first two. On the third, a Prius spins out of my way, and I see them, surging toward me from the north side of the intersection: more blue and red lights, more cop cars swerving to avoid civilian vehicles but clearly in hot pursuit of me. I scream and curse and gun it through the intersection, hurtling toward the harbor. I nearly clip the fender of a flashy red sports car, and the driver rolls down his window to shout curses at me, his words quickly lost to the wind.

Bright light illuminates the road in front of me, and I hear the steady drone of a helicopter's blades as it hovers above me. There's more shouting on a megaphone, but I can't make out the words over the revving of my engine and the rushing of my own blood. My rear-view mirror is filled with flashing blue and red lights.

I can see the harbor's lights now and the dark expanse of ocean water just past the docks, smooth like black glass. I've almost made it.

A police cruiser pulls out in front of me and comes to a dead stop across both eastbound lanes. I slam on the brakes, turning the wheel hard. My car slides until it's parallel to the cruiser, and when they make contact with the crunch of metal on metal, I look over to see the officer staring back at me is a woman about my age. We're only a few feet apart, separated by a pane of glass–her driver's side window, as my passenger side window has shattered, the seat filled with glass. She points her service revolver and shouts orders at me.

My car's engine is still running. "Please," I beg her, tears streaming down my face. "Please."

Her lips curl, her nostrils flare. And then she nods, almost imperceptibly, and lowers her weapon. My foot hits the accelerator, and I'm off again, skidding around her cruiser and hurtling toward the harbor.

There's a sharp sound that must be gunfire, and Tyler's car careens down the dock, the steering wheel jerking and leaping in my hands. Outside the driver's side window are quaint buildings advertising boat tours and warehouses probably filled with fish and other seafood harvested from the ocean. Outside my passenger side window, piers extend from the dock, each lit by a tall streetlight. Dozens of boats moored to the piers bob in the water. Everything looks hazy through my panic.

I count the piers until I arrive at number four. I slam my foot on the brake pedal, and the car screeches to a halt. Behind me, police cars do the same. Not one, not two, not three–Christ, five police cars, at least. Overhead, the helicopter illuminates my car with a spotlight. I wonder if there's a camera crew filming this, if Tyler's at home watching the news right now.

What is happening? When did my life become an action movie?

I want to freeze, all my instincts telling me not to move. But I have to, or I'm going to lose everything. If the police know I'm pregnant, they won't shoot at me, right? I fling open the car door and barrel out. Behind me, cops yell commands. Time slows to a crawl. To my right, on the pier, a shadowy figure motions me to a dinghy tied in the water.

Shots ring out. A bullet grazes my leg with a sensation like a bee sting, and I stumble, going to the ground. The spotlight glares down on me. The air is filled with the thumping of helicopter blades, the shouting of police officers and the screeching of tires as more backup arrives.

I'm going to die. I'm sure of it. They'll either shoot me now, or my monstrous offspring will chew its way out of me in a few months. I wish I'd spent more time traveling. I wish I hadn't given up playing the guitar. I wish I'd apologized to my mom for that fight we had. I pull myself to my feet and limp toward the pier. A bullet in the back now is better than being eaten alive tomorrow.

But there are no more bullets. The spotlight swings away from me. I turn to look as it glides over the ground and lands on a crowd of children running full-tilt toward me, emerging from behind the warehouses to tear down the dock with reckless speed. Behind me, the cops point their guns in my direction; before me, a horde of feral children approach at a rapid sprint, foaming at the mouth, making terrifying snarling sounds and snapping at the air with their small, sharp teeth. They claw at nothing as they run with fingers tipped in sharp, glinting fingernails. In the bright spotlight, I can see that one of them is the size of a four-year-old and has only one pigtail. There's something wrong with her mouth, and I realize with an icy drop in my stomach that she's eaten away her lips, leaving only ragged chewed-up flesh around her teeth and gums. And the long nails on her fingers aren't nails at all—they're the tips of her fingerbones.

Pity, fear, and revulsion boil inside me. Her eyes meet mine, and for just an instant, I think about her mother. Does she sit at home right this very second, sobbing, wondering whether she weeps out of relief or sorrow?

"Hurry!" the person on the dock yells.

Her voice galvanizes me to action, and I dash to the right, toward the boat, leaving the cops and the children to meet where I was standing. The cops open fire. The infected children know no pain; their nerve endings are as good as dead. They can only be stopped by a bullet to the brain. Cops don't want to shoot kids in the head and kill them—these days, that's a capital offense. They're taking body shots, and that does little to stop the onslaught. Screams echo across the water as the kids reach the officers, throwing themselves onto their victims with triumphant howls.

I race down the pier and clamber down a ladder into the metal boat. Three other women crouch there, staring at me wide-eyed. The pilot unties the ropes that moor us and jumps down into the boat with a grunt, making the dinghy slosh. She turns and pulls the ripcord for the motor. It sputters.

A child gallops on all fours down the dock toward us, screeching in animal excitement. I steel myself, grabbing an oar out of the bottom of the boat and preparing to defend us. My heart thunders in time with the feral child's loping steps, hitting the dock with a sound like a rapidly ticking metronome, *clomp clomp, clomp clomp.*

But the motor starts with a satisfying roar on the second pull, and the dinghy leaps from the pier and away with such alacrity it tips me over into the bottom of the boat. The child screams in fury, running back and forth along the pier and howling like a confused, rabid dog.

The other women help me to a sitting position. I turn to the woman steering the craft. "Kendra?"

"At your service," a familiar voice says, her face invisible with the lights of the pier behind her.

"What did you do to piss off the cops?" One of the other women huddled in the boat asks. We watch until the feral children and the police become too small to see anymore. The helicopter continues to circle with its searing light illuminating the fray, but the sounds of gunfire and the thump of the helicopter blades become distant, like a fading memory. The metallic reek of blood wafts across the open water to us and turns my stomach.

"I told my boyfriend where I was going and took his car," I answer. My insides feel scooped out and hollow, like there's only echoing where my organs used to be.

"Rookie mistake," one of the other women says, her tone sarcastic.

"You'll be wanted now," the first woman says breathily.

"Better than dead," I reply. Tears cascade down my face. My old life is gone. Where will I go now? I wish I could call Anna, or my mom.

"I'm wanted in three countries," Kendra says, and I can't see her face in the darkness, but I can hear the smile in her voice. "Most of the women on the *Ophelia* are wanted somewhere. It's a mark of pride for us. So, well done. And welcome to the sisterhood."

My heart does a backflip. As we glide across the water toward the yacht, I have a distinct sense this is the moment where my life will change completely, forever. But as I lower the oar back into the bottom of the boat and look at the terrified women crouching behind me, I think that maybe, just maybe, this might be exactly where I belong.

THREE MEETINGS OF THE PREGNANT MAN SUPPORT GROUP

By James Beamon

I meet with the other pregnant men on Thursdays. Our room at the civic center is between the recovering alcoholics and cancer survivors. We're currently at eleven now that Wallace shot himself.

The room tries to look like it's for any ol' support group. An institutional-sized coffee pot sits amid literature on a card table in the back. Both the coffee and the literature are rarely touched. And the room can't blend in; any fool can tell it's a pregnant man meeting. The ring of seats defines us.

We sit in student desks. The wraparound ones, where a hard, cream-colored plastic desktop is attached to an even harder blue plastic chair with chrome tubes connecting everything, chrome tubes for legs. These student desks were originally built for left-handed students. Now, they're ideal for pregnant men. We can lean into the desks to balance the weight disparity from our unearthly, distended right sides. In the later stages of skoick pregnancy, they're the only comfortable seats to be had anywhere.

The only thing I'm looking forward to is the student desk when I arrive for the meeting. I hobble-waddle into the room, my left arm hanging like an anchor, my right resting on the bulbous curve blooming out of my side. I halfway slide, halfway collapse into the seat with a sigh. I'm the fourth one to arrive.

"Nick." Jamal greets me with a nod. He's fourteen months in—the risky time. "Hard day?"

I lean into the desk to find a good position, holding my cheek with my hand, as if his question about my comfort is the most fascinating subject I've ever heard. "I can't remember the last time a day's been easy," I reply.

"Speak for yourself, young'un," Master Chief says, also leaning in his seat. We call him Master Chief on account of the thirty years he gave the Navy. It fits his personality better than Chester Farnum. He's the oldest man here, at fifty-five, currently ten months pregnant, like me.

"I danced all the way here," he says, flashing the biggest smile. "I swear the sidewalk lit up like I was Michael Jackson."

We all laugh. It must be military conditioning that keeps him smiling, able to joke through the suck. Me, I count the time until I can get this thing cut out of me. One hundred seventy-six more days.

"Don't get him started," Carson says, adjusting his wire-rimmed glasses. He sits erect, bulgeless. Carson's one of the two postnatals left in the group and has taken it upon himself to chair the meetings in the weeks since Wallace. He points at Master Chief. "Here I thought you were growing an alien in your appendix, but apparently that hump on your side is just you full of shit."

We all laugh some more, which only makes my lungs and stomach hurt, which for some reason makes me laugh even harder.

The other guys start to trickle in. Plumber Dan and Judah Ahlborn hobble-waddle in together, followed by Miguel, our other resident postnatal. Ryan Crisp and Syed come next. We're at two empty seats, and Carson's saying, "Let's get started," when the new kid, Aaron, hurries in. I scarcely remember the days I could hurry. He's still able to wear jeans and a leather jacket instead of sweats, at four months, barely showing.

The postnatals rise, and the rest of us shimmy out of the desks. We start every meeting reciting the mantra.

"I am one of the few, one of the chosen. This experience will never come again. I choose to enjoy my life supporting life. I choose the fellowship of my brothers around me. I am still me, yet more. I will always remember, while I host another life, my life is still my own."

Perhaps it's force of habit, but we all look at the remaining empty seat while we pledge, the one Wallace made empty.

"Okay," Carson says, as we navigate back into our desks. "So, who wants to start?"

When he says "start," what he means is who wants to continue? Continue unloading all the bullshit heaped on us since the last week. Ryan Crisp, carrying heavy bags under his blue eyes and seven months of gestating alien organism, raises his hand.

"I got fired from the gym today. I guess folding towels and sitting at the front desk are too strenuous for a pregnant personal trainer."

"They can't do that," Carson says, shaking his head. "Sue those clowns for discrimination."

Ryan shakes his head. "They made firing my ass a whole presentation: slides, executives in suits that came from corporate, the works. They showed me quarterly earnings for a full year, projected earnings, quotas, subscription rates, and a bunch of other trash. It was their way of saying, 'We're not earning enough money, we can prove it, and we're cutting you because you're a personal trainer who can't train anybody and the ones who can'll fold the towels now, thanks.'"

He barks a terse laugh. "The funny thing is, I can't even blame them. While I was sitting at the front desk, people would come into the gym, see me, and turn right back around. Then there were the ones who walked around me like they were afraid any second this thing'd burst out of me and wrap around their faces. It was easy for them to show me their profit loss, because I caused it."

Ryan shrugs. The defeated look on his face is familiar at these meetings. "I'll be all right. It wasn't like I was making a mint. Personal trainers get paid mostly off commission from client sessions, and I had none. The government stipend takes care of the rent, and Kuumbarura makes sure I have some walking-around money. I don't need the gym."

"Fuck 'em," Master Chief grunts.

"Woo, woo," we all chant, banging our fists twice on the desks.

We go around the room, airing new complaints, re-airing old ones that still feel fresh. Plumber Dan still can't get a work contract. Judah Ahlborn's father is still a dick. "Unsightly" is how his father describes him, which may be an improvement from the "living blasphemy" Judah was a few months ago. Syed has to stay in the back of his own restaurant; otherwise, the customers get squeamish about the food. Most days, he doesn't go at all because at twelve months it's hard to navigate the narrow confines of the kitchen, and some of the staff literally burn themselves giving him a wide berth.

The new kid, Aaron, raises his hand tentatively.

"People here have been calling me 'crabmeat.' I mean, back in Iowa, it would've been 'alien whore' if I had stuck around long enough to show. That's what they called pregnant dudes on TV. Here they say 'crabmeat.'" Aaron looks around the room with the question on his face. "Why is that?"

We all look at each other. I thought everyone knew at this point. Didn't he have a doctor trained in xenobiology for his quinquemesterly checkups who explained all this?

How do you tell somebody their pregnancy is little more than playing host to a mind-controlling parasite?

"'Cause, we look like we would walk better if we did it sideways, like a crab," Jamal says.

No one else speaks. Apparently, the answer to the question I posed in my head was to lie. As the kid nods slowly in acceptance, I feel my indignation rising. I lean toward Aaron.

"Fuck that."

"C'mon now," Carson starts. I raise a hand to silence him.

"If you're gonna chair, Carson, keep us honest. We all got enough to shoulder. Last thing we need is to come here to lie to each other. Hell, don't we spend enough time lying to ourselves?"

I turn my attention back to Aaron.

"Scientists have studied skoick pregnancy, and the closest thing they can compare it to here is a barnacle called Sacculina. When a female Sacculina locates a suitable host, most often the green shore crab, she looks for a joint in the crab's shell. When she finds it, she sheds her own shell and—zip!—injects herself into the crab."

Confusion clouded his features. "But there's no he's or she's with the Sko'ickari. They're nonbinary."

"Not the point, Aaron. The point is, the barnacle invades the crab, and once she's in there, she develops a root system with tendrils shooting into the crab's major organs: the stomach, the intestines. The brain. At that point, the Sacculina takes over the crab's mind, forces it to take care of her."

"You're saying the skoick fetus in my appendix is also in my brain, making me do things?" Aaron asks. He looks around the room. "And y'all believe that? The thing's four months old."

Carson jumps in. "Look, all Nick's saying is, soon you'll have urges you can't explain and can't understand and maybe not even fight. You won't want to fight them at the time. We don't want you to freak out. It's a natural part of this process."

"As natural as artificial flavor!" Master Chief says with his usual smile. "But yeah, don't let us scare you. No reason to climb out on a ledge or get depressed. Just roll with the punches. And don't neglect your housework; clean your dishes, floors, and toilets."

Aaron looks around at all the bigger-bellied men and nods. I guess company is one of the perks of the support group. If nothing else, you can see you're not the only one going through some out of this world weird shit. We're what misery loves.

Carson looks at me. "Something you want to share, Nick?"

I shrug. "Not especially."

"Your birthing partner's leaving for Sko'icka this week, isn't ne?"

I smile dryly. "Good of you to remember."

His voice softens like a purring whisper. "It'll be fine. It's a part of the process, too. It's okay."

Before Wallace ended himself, he used to do this same shit. Carson's not talking to me but past me, to what's in me. If it bothered me seeing Wallace do it to the other guys before, I really hate it now that I'm the one being talked through.

"I actually don't mind," I growl.

I swear I mean it.

Also, I knew it was a stupid idea to come this week. I shouldn't have listened to my sister.

I let Kim know when she picks me up.

"None of them listened. Those dudes spent fifteen full minutes consoling the unborn alien baby through my tough, guarded exterior."

"Tsk." She clicks her tongue with a shake of her head. "If only they spent twenty minutes. You would've broke like a window at the batting cages."

We both laugh a bit, her leaning one arm out the window, me leaning simply to breathe a bit easier. At least she gets me. I don't have to advertise I'm joking. She believes me when I tell her something.

"So," she says, "what are you going to do with your time now that Seqanen's leaving?"

I shrug. "Everything I've been doing minus the extra-tingly, mind-blowing interspecies sex."

Kim drives in silence for a spell. "So...like my life then."

No one knows why the Sko'ickari only choose men to carry their babies. It's the appendix the fetuses are inserted in, not the Adam's apple. I shudder at the thought of the alternative and how that would look ten months in.

That said, skoick–female relationships are rare, a novelty in which the skoick partner won't even attempt to procreate. The skoicks don't deem it necessary to explain this, or anything else, really. And the world governments don't care enough to ask, just in case being too nosy compromises the trade agreement. X number of human birthing hosts for Y amount of advanced alien technology per year.

Kim pulls up to my apartment building. "Same time next week," she announces.

"No." I give her the same answer I gave her last week.

"Sounds like a date," she replies.

Seqanen is still packing when I get inside the apartment. There is nothing high tech or futuristic about the process. Two legs walking about the place with two hands grabbing things to place in a suitcase. The suitcase is cool-looking: a bright orange, durable polymer material, but we were making these ourselves before the skoicks showed up.

Skoicks are seven-fingered. The digits grow longer as they get further away from the thumb; the universe's way of confirming our pinkies are useless. Their everything angles upward. Their eyes look like teardrops, noses like rising arrowheads. Hairless, their heads curve to resemble a flame frozen in time.

Seqanen stands a foot taller than me. Like humans, skoicks come in different colors. Mine is red. Ne is wearing a blue *gindara*, a traditional skoick outfit that resembles an evening gown. The *gindara* stands in beautiful contrast to nir strawberry-hued skin.

"You're home," ne says with a smile. "I'm glad. I've nearly finished preparing, so we won't have any distractions."

The sight of nem placing things in the suitcase triggers emotions I'm sure aren't mine. My body isn't my own when it rushes over, falls at nir feet and wraps my arms around nir legs.

My head shakes. My voice says, "Don't go. Don't go."

I feel Seqanen's fingers through my hair, on my neck. It is calming.

"I must leave and build. My child can't survive without a nest."

My head continues to shake vigorously.

Seqanen says nothing more. Ne simply hums and strokes my hair. Eventually, the fear subsides, my muscles unlock, and I can stand.

"Why me?" I ask nem.

"I chose you," ne replies.

"I'm not a Pikachu! That's not an answer. Why me?"

Ne chews on the question a while, long lashes batting. Those eyes. I swear they each contain universes onto themselves.

"This is that thing between our cultures that I feel I cannot explain. I did not pick you but rather chose. 'Chose' is the only word your language has for it. But I've always chosen you, will always choose you. It is written in the stars."

I don't know how to respond. At ten months pregnant, it's a little too late to say much of anything anyway.

Seqanen smiles. "I know what will cheer you up."

Ne holds up nir fingers. They throb as they grow, elongate, split. Soon, each appendage is many-tendrilled like a cat o' nine tails, with small nodes along their lengths that resemble the pods of a Venus fly trap.

I undress with thirsty abandon. Seqanen steps closer to me. The tendrils wrap around my chest and back, my neck, my legs. They snake up from my neck onto my face, into my nose and ears. One wraps around my shaft. Another snakes its way inside.

Ne opens nir mouth. Nir tongue has elongated and budded like nir fingers. I part my lips and accept these tendrils on my tongue, down my throat.

Everywhere the nodes touch radiate joy. It's like human nerves can barely process it, like simultaneously experiencing the joyful release of orgasm and the shuddery satisfaction of the moments after at the same time.

Maybe this is why the skoicks almost exclusively choose men. If we were known to have been led by our dicks before, this kind of feeling could lead a man right off a suspension bridge.

In the morning, Seqanen's gone. Ne will spend the next five months on Sko'icka, shedding skin and secreting fluids to build the perfect post-human habitat for nir child. I don't experience any other breakdowns or episodes. And Thursday comes.

This time, Kim doesn't have to work as hard to get me to the meeting. I hobble-waddle into the room and slide into the student desk, an ill-fitting glove, but the only glove ever made for a misshapen hand. The two remaining postnatals, Carson and Miguel, are talking to each other near the coffee. Jealousy flashes, seeing them stand tall and erect, holding their Styrofoam cups. Look at them, just a couple of normal dudes. They could walk, not hobble, away from this room and fit in anywhere. Once I reached that stage, no way would I be here hanging out with a bunch of side-swollen crybabies.

Half the guys are already here: Jamal, Master Chief, Plumber Dan. Judah Ahlborn, Syed, and Ryan Crisp come in shortly after me. We stand and give our mantra to Wallace's empty chair. The kid, Aaron, has yet to arrive.

Master Chief dives right in.

"Fellas," he says, "just like our boy, Nick, here, my baby's leaving me. I tried to convince her to take me with her, but she ain't hearing me. She told me our kid's too underdeveloped for interstellar travel."

Master Chief had apologized to us all the first couple of meetings about being old school. There was no "ne" or "nem" for Master Chief, no using "nir" instead of her. He had always dated a woman before this; as far as he was concerned, gender-neutral language and PC attitude could go to hell.

Unlike me last week, Master Chief seems to welcome the consolations and condolences that come from the other guys. We go around the room, where Jamal reminds us with a smile that he's two weeks away from a neat trip to Sko'icka and the title of postnatal. In other news, Judah Ahlborn's dad is still a cockbite, but Plumber Dan finally found some work.

Aaron finally walks into the room while Plumber Dan is describing the weird, awkward angles he has to turn to get at the pipes underneath the sink. Aaron plops into the seat, looking like he's a thousand miles away. The look instantly kills Plumber Dan's talk about P-traps.

A few moments into the newfound silence, Aaron, looking down, speaks to his student desk.

"I drank from the toilet," he says.

I say nothing.

"After I used it, I got up, and I looked at the water and shit swirl down. The new water was filling the bowl and something in my head made that rising water seem like it was the most refreshing beverage I'd ever taste, and I absolutely had to drink it. Then I was there, on all fours, head in the bowl, goddamn drinking."

Aaron looks up from the desk and finds my eyes.

"Is that what you mean by mind control? Crabmeat?"

I nod. "Your baby is learning to drive human. Until it gets a better handle, it'll drive on instinct."

The traditional skoick host is an ignaruuk, a four-legged, sloth-looking creature that never evolved into sentience like the skoicks. The fetuses instinctually know how to compel the four-legged beasts, and a hundred thousand years of hardwired evolutionary behavior wasn't going to change overnight because the skoicks found what they believe are better hosts.

"Why would I want it to get a better handle?" Aaron said. "Why would I want it driving any part of me?"

"It'll keep you from drinking out of the toilet," I reply.

Master Chief leans toward Aaron. "I hope you listened when I told you to stay on your housework."

Aaron looks around the room as if we all betrayed him. "This has happened to, what? All of you?"

None of us nod, but none of us shake our heads either.

"But Bereksid never said any of this to me! Ne never said it would take over my body when ne asked my permission. What about the Dreamcall?"

Every now and then, one of us would put on our nostalgia glasses and talk about the Dreamcall. Invariably, they're all the same, where our specific skoick birthing partner first appears to us in a dream. They bat their eyes that contain the whole universe in them at us and tell us they need us.

"It was just a dream," I tell Aaron. "Just a call."

No one knows if the Dreamcall is something the skoicks can do naturally or sort of advanced technology. The skoicks pick and choose what tech they share with our world, and Dreamcalling hasn't hit the access list yet.

"Oh, my God," Aaron says as he shakes his head. "Just... oh, my God." He takes off abruptly. Carson takes off after him.

We all look at each other, unsure of how to proceed. I know one thing for sure—Aaron gives me plenty to talk about when Kim picks me up.

"It was strange, Sis," I tell her, leaning toward her as she drives. "I don't think he has a doctor. It doesn't seem like he's done a lick of research on what his condition means or what to expect."

"I remember first time you chugged the bowl," Kim says. "That was before you converted to cleanliness as a lifestyle.

You remember how your toilet used to have a dirt ring?"

"I don't have to remember," I tell her. "I can still taste it."

We both laugh. For a few moments, there's only the sound of her car motor as we move through the city. Kim spares a serious glance at me.

"You remember what you told me the day after?"

"I'm pretty sure I said, 'If I could find a way to get this thing out of me, I'd jump on it.'"

"There's a guy. I hear he's a doctor who got his license pulled," Kim says. "Pissed off the government and medical community with his views on skoick invasiveness. I hear he maybe helps guys like you, Nick."

I raise my eyebrow. "Really?"

"Yeah, unlike most doctors, he realizes you can't walk into his office on your own two feet and say the A word. He understands that if a man appeared in his office unconscious because the man's sister drugged him, and then she and her husband carry-dragged him there, well, that's as good as informed consent for that doctor."

"Yes," I tell her. Back when Seqanen first Dreamcalled, ne didn't explain the terms, how long I'd be this way, the things I'd be forced to do, none of this shit. Ne just exuded nir need, this crushing need that even I could feel while ne looked at me with the eyes of the world's saddest puppy. I couldn't say no to that, and no matter how I try to look at it, I can't help but feel manipulated—mind controlled—even from the start. Yes, abort this thing.

"No," my mouth says a moment later.

"No?" Kim asks. "This second thoughts or second opinion?"

"No abortion. I want nem to grow."

"Okay, no it is," Kim says. She says nothing else for the few minutes it takes to get me to my apartment. As I grab the door handle, Kim grabs my other wrist.

"You want me to come up, make you some tea? Remember how you used to like Sleepytime? I could make you some of that."

I never liked Sleepytime. I snatch my wrist away.

"I said no! I want nem. I'm keeping nem. You're just jealous of us, watching nem grow while you have no child. You'll never have a child. You'll always be barren. No, I don't want your help, jealous and barren. No."

A moment later, the things I said hurt my heart. "Kim..." I begin.

"Get out." Her hand, the one I snatched away from, is shaking violently.

"Kim..."

"Go!"

Reluctantly, I listen and watch her as she peels off. I head into my apartment, which seems drab and colorless now that Seqanen's gone. My career field is IT, configuring firewalls and doing penetration testing, which was a work-from-home job even before the pregnancy. I don't have the same weekly work struggles as many of the guys, but I also don't have anything to distract me from my lifeless apartment. I don't even know if I have family anymore.

I dab the moisture forming in my eyes. That kind of thing's not going to help anybody. I call Kim and apologize when it goes to voice mail. I call again and apologize to voice mail again. I send her flowers. Then a gift card. Then another voice mail apology. Then, an e-card with a fun animation that took me hours to find.

Four days into my campaign, Kim calls me.

"You know, there are less expensive ways to get to your meetings. Uber picks you up anywhere."

"Uber?! Why take my chances with a potentially crazy driver when I get a verifiably crazy driver?"

The silence hangs between us for a moment.

"I'm sorry."

"I know. Shut up. I'll see you on Thursday."

True to her word, Kim shows up Thursday, smiling as if nothing ever happened. God bless, I want to hug her, but she's in the car already and hugging at this stage is awkward. Instead, I lean toward her even more from the passenger seat and kiss her cheek.

"That better not be toilet-water lips," she says.

Because of an accident on the highway, I'm the last one to arrive. Even Aaron's here before me. Apparently, they've already spoken the mantra, and Jamal has the floor. He's using his time to freak everyone out.

"I don't want to get cut open. I think it'll be better if I stay where I am."

This is why the fourteenth month is the risky time. The young skoick has mastered the human neural network enough to process the fact that soon someone will cut it away from the only home it's ever known but not enough awareness to understand this is in its best interest. There's been reports of fourteen-monthers running away from home, where they die as the skoick child bursts their appendix, lungs, and whatever else breaking through the skin to get to open air. Just like the traditional sloth-like ignaruuk, birthing skoicks is a lethal process for the host.

"I know it's scary," Carson says, speaking more through Jamal than to him. "Trust me, I've been there. But it doesn't hurt. And the infant can't survive for long without the nest. Ne can survive eating your organs for two days or so before the meat spoils and becomes unpalatable. Ne needs the nest."

Jamal takes a few calming breaths. He nods.

"You should call the skoick embassy," Carson adds. "Tell them what happened at this meeting. Let them know it's time."

As Jamal nods confirmation, Aaron raises his hand.

"Jamal should wait. This isn't all that's happening with this meeting." From his leather jacket pocket, Aaron pulls a pistol.

The other eight pregnant men, me included, instinctively reach and cover our bulging sides with both arms. The sight makes Aaron laugh.

"Y'all don't even have enough of your own mind left to cover your face or just rock back or something. No, all your energy, everything you've got, spent protecting the parasite."

No one says a word as Aaron looks around the room. "You know why the skoicks don't try this shit with women?" The revolver swivels toward each of us in turn. "Because they're built to carry life naturally. Their bodies aren't going to let this abomination grow in their appendix like a disease while their womb is lying dormant. But, dudes? We never see it coming. Haha! Like being robbed at gunpoint."

Through the fear, I put one hand up to Aaron. "No need for the gun. It's none of our faults. We can't help this."

"Don't you think I know that, Nick?" Aaron looks around the room at the other pregnant men. "What I'm saying is, I'm here to help this. Apparently, I can't help myself. I've been trying to help myself all week. Seems you need to be a postnatal, like Wallace, before your body'll let you swallow a bullet. But there's no reason I shouldn't be able to help you guys. That's why I'm here—to help you all."

Aaron points the gun at me, the dead center of my bulging side. He stares at it, hatred in his eyes. The gun's dark barrel seems to gape open like the maw of the abyss. Aaron's steady hand quivers. His brow furrows. The gun-hand shakes. And shakes. And shakes.

He lowers the gun. His eyes fill up with tears.

"Even that, too," he whispers.

Carson gets up, hugs the scared kid sitting in the student desk. The gun falls out of Aaron's hand as he grips fistfuls of Carson's shirt and bawls like a lost infant.

The meeting doesn't last much longer after this. The guys come here to unload, not to strap on more trauma to carry home. I'm sure Judah Ahlborn would take a jerk dad over a desperate kid waving a gun every day of the week, including Thursdays.

The guys slowly trickle out. My sister's held up in a department store across town, so I've got time to kill. Soon, there's only Carson and me.

"Poor kid," I say. "Hard to come to terms with choice being taken away."

Carson shrugs. "I don't think he ever had a choice to begin with. Even before the Dreamcall."

"What do you mean?"

"You know the skoicks don't have a word for choice?" he asks. "My former birthing partner explained to me that they understand our word 'choice' as this murky area between pick and force."

"Pick is the same thing as choose."

He shakes his head. "Not to them. A pick is an arbitrary selection. What items you put on your plate at an all-you-can-eat buffet, which random numbers you highlighted on a losing lottery ticket, those are picks. Even those forced into conditions have picks. A slave with the option of two shirts from his meager closet. The choice of chicken or fish when you're flying on an airplane, held captive thirty thousand feet above the ground. To them, choice is much different."

"So, what is it? What's choice to them?"

"That's the thing I don't think they know how to really explain. I don't think they see choice as a choice. The things that impact our lives in meaningful ways have already been decided to skoicks, and they're just waiting for time to catch up, to reveal the results."

I look up at the ceiling. "It's written in the stars."

He takes his glasses off and rubs the bridge of his nose. For the first time, I notice how tired he looks, more so now than when he was carrying a skoick.

"Why do you do it?" I ask him. "You're done. Fifteen months paid. Why do you come back and chair these meetings?"

He puts his glasses back on. A smirk plays across his face. "There's purpose in it. I suppose I need that."

There must not be much sense of purpose in it. As Aaron pointed out, Wallace shot himself once he had control of his body again. Chairing these meetings didn't seem to have helped him all that much.

I realize that I've been so busy cursing the experience of carrying the fetus and counting the days that I haven't really contemplated what it meant to be postnatal. I figured life was so much better for these guys that I didn't stop to wonder if it really was.

"How do you feel?" I ask Carson. "You know, after the full fifteen months, the months after. Hell, after this gun scare. How do you typically feel?"

He stares at me for a moment. "You really want to know?"

I nod.

He looks off into space, his eyes dancing as he considers the question. For the briefest of moments, I see the whole universe contained in his eyes.

"Empty," he says.

LETTER FROM OHIO 2025

By Zoë Brigley

Do you remember those afternoons in summer? The high and tight sound: that ratta-tatta-tatta of the sprinklers making arcs over the grass? You joked that our lawn was the worst in the neighborhood. Before long, the home-owner's association did send a letter out, said we had X number of days to turn our green patch into monoturf—a luminous, plastic carpet.

It's all yellow now. Water quotas mean yellow lawns, and yellow clay exposed with great cracks in it. I swear I can feel the foundations of the house shifting, squeezed by the dry earth.

I never thought we should live here—a part of the country that was once overgrown woodland, now sterile fields. The Wyandot, or Huron, lived here first, pushed out from Georgian Bay in Canada. They lived in longhouses in tight-knit villages, but when the white settlers came, they brought a new name: Great Dismal Swamp. They drained it, mowed down trees for fields, forced it to bear crops. That's how it's been ever since: fighting the land into sub-mission, always at war with the insects, the weeds, the mold that blights the plants, and the poison sumac drilling its tap root deep into the ground.

Years have passed since you disappeared, and they tell me now that it's time to forget you. The boys are so tall and long you would hardly recognize them. Jon is in fourth grade, studying hard on his math, and Thomas lost his round babyface when he started kindergarten. Every night,

I sit in the rocking chair, and read to them. We started *Alice Through the Looking Glass*, but I had to leave off because it gave me a peculiar feeling. How she looks into the mirror, and sees it all—everything reversed, and back to front, not how it should be at all.

They are pressuring me to marry again, but I continue to persuade; I can't marry another man if my husband is still alive. Marriage is sacrosanct now. It's supposedly a woman's duty to marry as soon as possible and have children. I could tell them that the more people there are, the worse things will be, but they wouldn't listen. All they want is more young minds to fashion in their own image.

So many of their rules are supposed to save us from global warming, but it's just an excuse. It's actually about control. None of it makes sense; they want more babies, but there are strict rules about how we have sex. No sex before marriage, no abortions, and no contraception. Abstinence saves the unborn, they tell us, but that's just for the unmarried.

The other day, they sent a new man round to check the energy meters. Straight away, there was something I disliked about him. Maybe it was his doughy face, or the cool, flat flesh of his fingers when he shook my hand. His name—Mike—was stitched in white letters on the chest pocket of his blue boiler suit. He had a mild-mannered voice, but I could tell he was a true believer...

"Is that you?" Mike asked, pointing at our wedding photo. I nodded wordlessly. "I'm sorry about your husband. A lot of folks got shaken up in the mix when they closed state borders. It has to be done to keep us safe, but it's a shame for you. Still young enough to have another baby, too."

"I'm done having children," I say.

"I'd be careful about saying things like that," he said. "We all have our duties. It must be hard for you here by yourself. It doesn't look like your husband maintained the house and garden very well."

"Oh, he never liked yard work much," I replied. "I had to nag him to get jobs done, or do them myself."

"You see," he said, "what you oughta have done was to put out a long glass of lemonade, and make a game of it. And after he did the work, if he wanted something a bit more than lemonade, well..."

Fuck off, Mike, I think. But I don't know how much longer I'll be able to avoid it. You know if it happens, it won't be my choice.

If you are out there somewhere, I hope you are thinking about me, and the kids. I didn't know that the clamp-down would come that week when I took them up to the cabin. I didn't know that when I drove back, you'd be gone.

I have to admit I was angry at first, and scared. It was too late for us to leave then. Perhaps I should have driven out of the state when I heard the news on the car radio, but I was thinking of you. The phone lines were jammed, and I couldn't leave without you.

Yes, I really was angry, but I've thought about it since. I can imagine you running the numbers with that rational brain of yours, seeing that the obvious answer was for you to leave right then. Maybe you thought that I would do the same, and we would meet up somewhere. Maybe you thought that if you got out, you could reach us later, help us do the same. Why didn't we see this coming with the first abortion ban? Why didn't we leave when we had the chance?

Sometimes, I wonder if you were just a coward, leaving us behind. I could forgive you that, though. Much worse is the thought that you were hurt, because there were "accidents" around that time. I tried emailing Anchita but never heard back, and I only have a pass to drive in our neighborhood. I wondered about what happened to her and the kids down in the city. Sometimes, in my worst moments, I imagine you dead. I think the boys wonder, too, but we don't speak it out loud.

Meanwhile, the state lawmakers tell us we must live

and work locally, and women are encouraged to stay at home for the most part. Stay local for the planet's survival. Women work as nurses or secretaries, but hardly any bother. They pay us womenfolk to stay at home, and I'm not sure that I want to be out there in this new world. They are marrying young women off as quick as they can. "Mama bears protect the home" goes the slogan.

Sometimes I imagine you back here with me. The other day, I was spraying insecticide around the base of the house, trying to keep the swarms at bay, when I came upon a pebble that we brought back years ago from a trip to the Virginia coast. Remember, before we had children, how we stayed out there in a cabin by the beach for weeks, so balmy that we lived in (or out of) our swimsuits. My hair turned wavy from the seawater, I swam so much, and we slept curled up to one another. I miss your body. Not your young body from when we first met, but your thirty-something body from the last time I saw you. The strong, broad chest of you.

If you were here, though, I don't know how we would manage. I can't imagine that we'd want to bring any more children into the world. And to put two people in a marriage together, where sex is only for making babies, might be a kind of torture. I suspect, though, that people find a way, as they always have. In the past, people made condoms out of silk paper, lamb intestines, or soaked linen. There are ways around the rules—for the unmarried kids desperate to discover each other, for the married ones who don't want any more children. They would be in trouble if they were found out, but no one can be in our bedrooms watching, or at least not for now.

I have to tell you that it's hard without you. I know you always thought I was so strong, but now I'm scared. If I never get out of here, I doubt that I'll ever see you again. When the push comes, I will have to leave, but then there's the children. I make plans. I gather maps. It might have to be on foot, my best route being over the hills and mountains to Pennsylvania. I'll leave on a Friday after I pick up Thomas and Jon from school, so they might not notice we're gone until Monday. I'm just not sure if Thomas can manage it yet, so in the meantime, I play the dutiful mother and the grieving, abandoned wife.

That summer when I found you gone, and us all trapped here, I was so angry. I used to walk out onto the back patio wearing nothing but my bikini. I would lie out there all afternoon, hoping to make the lidless windows of suburban houses blink. I would lie there listening to sprinklers, their ratta-tatta-tatta, and when the wind blew, a fine mist would fall, glistening over my bare skin. By their own rules, nobody was allowed to touch me—a married woman. It was a small act of defiance, but I've changed since then.

No one is allowed to use the sprinklers now, and it is so quiet in the empty house while the boys are at school. Most days I stay inside, the blinds drawn against the blazing sun. If I make myself so very small, perhaps they might not notice me. If I keep myself small, perhaps they'll forget I exist.

IMPOSTER SYNDROME

By Michelle Renee Lane

I'd spent four months planning the trip to Melbourne. It took that much time to book a flight that fit within my budget, worked with my PTO days, and was timed just right for my COVID test to still be valid long enough to board the flight and not be quarantined to a hotel room for a week before even setting foot in the city. I wanted to have as much time as possible to spend visiting with Jack. I'd never met Jack in person. We'd only ever chatted online or through video calls on days when we couldn't rely on texting to share all the thoughts racing around in our heads.

I know what you're thinking. You're thinking that I'm crazy for flying to the other side of the world to meet someone who is essentially a stranger. Maybe I am crazy. Maybe not. Jack is one of the first people I'd met in a long time who I just seemed to click with automatically. He was kind. A little shy at first. But genuine. Authentic. Cool and funny, with a very dark sense of humor that bordered on morbid. I really liked him. In fact, over the two years we'd been talking, I'd grown to love him.

Love is a funny thing. You never know when it's going to sneak up on you and bite you on the ass. I'm not one of those lovesick women who chases after relationships hoping to find her happily ever after. While other girls were planning their weddings at recess in elementary school, I was playing smear the queer and climbing the monkey bars with the boys. Most of my closest friends are male. Some of my oldest friendships are with boys I grew up with who went on to have families and careers, and still liked catching up with me over drinks when we happened to be in the same geographical location. I had friendships with some of them that have lasted more than twenty years. And yet, I was about to turn forty and was still very single. Never married. No children. Not even a half-assed boyfriend to share the rent. Always a best friend but never a bride. Is that how the saying goes?

I know that isn't how it goes, but that version works much better for my set of circumstances. It's not that I wanted to be a bride. Becoming a wife wasn't on my list of top five goals. It didn't even make the top ten. But that didn't mean I wasn't looking for partnership. Connection. I'd had my share of half-assed boyfriends, lovers, and friends with benefits, and none of them ever grew into something more meaningful. Something that would last beyond the three- or four-year mark and coast into comfortable companionship. I wasn't necessarily bound by the rules of strict monogamy, but I at least wanted someone to look at me and think I was worth the effort to make me a priority without having to ask. I wanted to be someone's numero uno, their main squeeze, their lady. So far, that wasn't happening in my reality, and I was beginning to think that it never would.

After meeting Jack, I was hopeful again.

My flight landed at Melbourne Airport roughly thirty-four hours after boarding my first plane. It was a hot, sunny Monday afternoon in June when I flew out of Pittsburgh, and it was a cold, rainy Wednesday evening when I landed in Australia. I forgot about the difference in seasons between the two hemispheres and had packed for warmer weather. I felt like an idiot standing outside the airport waiting for a taxi, while sheets of rain soaked through my thin cotton sundress and ruined my tan leather sandals. Knowing I'd see Jack the next day was the only thing that kept me from crying in the frigid downpour.

When I awoke in my hotel room, it was dark. The clock on the bedside table said 6:00. But I couldn't tell if it was a.m. or p.m. The term 'jet lag' did not suitably cover the exhaustion and disorientation I was feeling. I didn't care what time it was. I was tired, so I went back to sleep. When I woke up again, the clock said 10:00, and it was light outside. I assumed it meant that it was morning, and I had plenty of time to shower, dress, and maybe even grab a bite to eat before Jack came by to pick me up for the afternoon.

He would have come sooner, but he didn't have anyone to look after his daughter until later in the day when her care worker started their shift. Being a single parent is difficult enough, but being the single parent of a child with special needs can seem insurmountable. At least that's what I had begun to understand through our conversations. His daughter, Anna, required round-the-clock care and couldn't be left alone. Apparently, soon after she was diagnosed with amyotrophic lateral sclerosis at the age of five, Anna's mother had a mental breakdown from all the stress of having a severely ill child. A month into caring for Anna, she left and never looked back. Jack had to figure out how to care for the girl on his own. It had been a struggle to get supports in place, find the resources to keep a roof over their heads, and maintain the strength to be the primary caregiver to a child who would always need full-time care. His struggle hadn't really ended. He'd just gotten better at accepting his fate.

Fate. Fate had helped me find Jack across all those miles, and now we were finally going to meet face-to-face. To say that I was nervous was an understatement. I knew he was attracted to me and that we were compatible, but I still worried about what he would think the first time he saw me in person. I spent an hour trying on outfits that weren't appropriate for the weather, and the funny thing was, I was certain he really wanted to see me in my birthday suit. The idea of being that close to him and remaining dressed seemed absurd. We'd been flirting and sexting for over a year, and now that we were finally going to be breathing the same air, all I could think about was getting him out of his clothes and getting him under me. Which meant I had to be comfortable enough with my own body to take my clothes off, too. That was no small feat. I hadn't been intimate with anyone for more than three years. According to him, he hadn't been with anyone in a lot longer than that. Exactly how long, I wasn't sure, but his daughter was eight, so you do the math.

I'd had enough sense to pack at least one pair of jeans. I put those on and a cotton shirt with short sleeves. Was there a cardigan at the bottom of my suitcase? No, but I did find a summer-weight hoodie, which was better than nothing. I hated the thought of buying warmer clothes, but I might have to pick up a few things if I wanted to be comfortable. Or maybe I'd just stay in bed with Jack the whole time and not worry about clothing at all. Of course, that wasn't possible, since he'd have to go home eventually and look after Anna.

Anna was bedridden, unable to walk, nonverbal, and had to have everything done for her. I imagined it was like having an infant that never developed past a certain stage but kept growing. I couldn't begin to imagine the emotional turmoil raging inside Jack, knowing that the only way he'd ever be free of his responsibilities would be for one of them to die. He wasn't a young man. He was older than me. Although children like Anna didn't typically have a very long life expectancy, she seemed to be clinging to life with a ferocity that often made him wonder if she'd outlive him. Sometimes, I think he secretly hoped he'd die first, even if that meant that strangers would be looking after her.

It was all very morbid and unsettling to think about. But those sorts of thoughts preoccupied him at times and made it difficult to relate to him when he'd get into a funk about his reality, and there'd be radio silence on his end for a few days until he could get a handle on his mental outlook. I couldn't blame him for feeling that way. Most people would. Parenting was a seemingly never-ending responsibility that most people knew would come to an end eventually, once their kids became a bit more self-sufficient and independent. There would be no independence for Anna.

After meeting Jack and learning about his daughter, I started reading up on ALS and, in a word, it was horrifying. To lose control of all your bodily functions over time and still be conscious of it happening to you. I couldn't think of too many other fates that were worse than death. This disease was definitely among the top three. I tried not to dwell on the sadder aspects of Jack's and Anna's lives while I waited for him in my hotel room. I'd ordered a pot of tea from room service in the hopes of warming myself up, and I had just poured myself a cup when there was a knock on the door.

Butterflies in my stomach made me queasy. My hands were sweating, and my heart raced. I couldn't remember the last time I felt so nervous.

There was another knock on the door. I couldn't wait forever to open it.

I breathed in through my nose and exhaled through my mouth. I checked myself in the mirror. Made sure I didn't have anything stuck in my teeth or sticking out of my nose, made sure both of my boobs were pointing in the same direction, said a little prayer under my breath, and opened the door.

Jack was much more handsome in person. He was tall and slender but not too skinny. There was some meat on his bones, and he had an aura of strength. I knew he liked to take long walks, but I wasn't sure if he did anything else to maintain his fitness. He stood in the doorway. Perfectly still. I watched him look at me. His gaze roved over every inch of me from head-to-toe, and I knew he liked what he saw. A smile slowly spread across his face, and his expression warmed me. Made me feel more relaxed. Safe.

"May I come in?"

"Please," I said, stepping aside.

He sat in the armchair next to the bed and stretched his legs out in front of him. I was happy to see him, but it was a little unnerving to see how easily he made himself at home in my room. Maybe it was all the fear and self-doubt talking. Or maybe my intuition was trying to tell me something. As usual, I ignored it.

"Tea?" I held up the pot.

"Love some." He folded his hands neatly in his lap.

"How do you take it?"

"Black with two sugars," he said.

I took mine with cream and two sugars.

"So," I said, blowing on the surface of the hot tea, "what's the plan for today?"

He took a sip of his tea and winced before setting the cup down again. "If you're hungry, we can grab some lunch and then do a little sightseeing before I take you home to meet Anna."

I wasn't sure if I'd be meeting Anna on this trip. Jack hadn't exactly been clear about what the expectation would be. I had assumed that we'd just spend time together, since he was always saying how much he needed a break. But if he trusted me enough to meet his daughter, I was happy to do so.

"That sounds lovely," I said.

After lunch, we took a walking tour with local street artists and saw some amazing graffiti, some of which was created by the people giving the tour. I wondered if there were any cities in the States that did that. I could think of a few that should. It was a brilliant way to support the arts in underserved communities, and it was an untapped source of tourism dollars. I made a mental note to bring it up at the next staff meeting at the non-profit where I worked.

The board would love the idea. I must have been lost in my thoughts, because Jack was staring at me with a slightly annoyed look on his face.

"I'm sorry, did you say something?"

"I said your name three times. Where did you wander off to in your head?"

I explained my idea, and he said he was happy to have provided the inspiration.

We took a taxi across town to an old prison that gave tours on the history of incarceration in Victoria, and some of the history included ghost stories about inmates that continued to haunt the prison for more than one hundred years. It was a great tour, and I learned a lot about the history of the place through the lens of criminal activity and the penal system.

After the tour, Jack took me to a bar for drinks and a snack. We'd been walking for hours. My feet were tired, and I was losing steam. Even though I'd slept for more than ten hours, I was still adjusting to the time difference and the long journey I'd taken to get there. We had a few drinks and talked about the different things happening in our lives. Caught each other up and sat in comfortable silence while we rested for a bit longer.

"Do you like rollercoasters?" he said out of the blue.

I laughed. "I haven't ridden one in a long time, but yeah. I like rollercoasters."

"Then our next stop is Luna Park."

"It's a bit cold to ride a rollercoaster," I said, regretting once again my choice of clothing for the trip.

He wrapped an arm around my shoulders and pulled me tight against him. "I'll keep you warm."

Aside from accidentally bumping into me a few times during our walking tours, this was the first real physical contact Jack had made with me. Maybe he was being a gentleman, but it struck me as odd, given the nature of our communication up to meeting face-to-face. Once again, the voices of self-doubt spoke up. What if he wasn't as attracted to me now that he'd met me in person? What if, after spending time with me, he decided the connection just wasn't working for him? If things didn't work out, I could spend the next ten days sightseeing on my own. Or try to get an earlier flight home.

"Are you ready to go?" His arm was still wrapped around my shoulders.

"Sure," I said, and finished my drink. "I just need to use the restroom first."

Forty-five minutes later, I was sitting at the crest of the first hill in the car of a wooden rollercoaster about to drop over the edge. I hadn't been on a rollercoaster in nearly twenty years, and now that I was about to go plummeting into the first turn and loop, I was questioning my logic around riding an amusement park ride that was built in the 1920s with a man I barely knew in a country I'd never visited before. I mean, I liked adventure as much as the next person, but at the moment, my emotional state and safety were in the hands of a stranger on a literal rollercoaster. I'm sure I'd look back on this moment one day and laugh. In about two seconds, I'd start screaming.

Screaming can be therapeutic at times. A deep soul cleanse. An exorcism of all the emotional energy we ignore. The feelings we pretend not to have. A scream, like a good cry, can release all that pent-up energy. Screaming can act like a reset button when you've been feeling stuck or uncertain about what path you should be on. Screaming has the potential to give you the clarity you need to choose which way to start walking when you find yourself at a crossroads.

I'd been staring at a crossroads for a long time and hadn't even realized it until I met Jack. He offered possibilities. New experiences. New adventures. Now he was sitting next to me, our bodies pressed close together and strapped down in a wooden car that was about to hurtle into space. And I was going to release my demons through a little impromptu shout therapy. When the car finally tipped over the edge of the track to begin its rapid descent toward Earth, a scream so deep and primal ripped out of my throat that it brought tears to my eyes. I continued to scream through the entire ride, which lasted fewer than three minutes. At the end of the ride, my body relaxed. I was spent like I'd just experienced a bone-rattling orgasm. I was at peace. Content. Dare I say, happy?

When the ride lurched to a complete stop, Jack wrapped his arms around me and kissed me deeply. He was clearly aroused. Excited. "Your screams made my cock rock hard," he said in a whisper against my ear.

A more sensible woman would have been mildly concerned about his statement. At the very least, I should have asked what, specifically, about my screams was a turn on. Was it a sensual sound, or was fear his kink? Instead of asking for clarity, I kissed him back and allowed myself to live in the moment.

After picking up his car at the hotel and driving for roughly two hours outside of the city, Jack pulled up to the front of his house.

"We're home," he said.

His home. Not my home. I dreamed of having my own home one day. I'd probably never be able to afford one on my meager salary. Hell, I'd used half my savings to be able to take this trip. The only way I'd ever have a home was if I met someone who wanted to live with me. Either I'd move into their home, or we'd buy one together. The possibility of that happening was becoming less and less likely as the years passed. I didn't know Jack well enough to even consider the idea of moving in with him. And once I returned to the States, I had no idea if or when I'd ever see him again.

My thoughts were interrupted by him opening the

passenger side door. I stepped from the car and noticed he was holding a suitcase. The suitcase I'd left in my hotel room.

"Why do you have my suitcase?"

"You'll be more comfortable here with me and Anna. I took care of your hotel bill for the one night and canceled the rest of your reservation. One of the staff packed your bag and put it in the boot of my car," he said.

"How...?"

"I left my car parked in the hotel garage while we were sightseeing. It was easy for them to take care of it."

"I wish you would have asked me."

"I thought you'd want to spend more time together while you're here. This way, you can meet Anna and I can be at home to look after her," he said, carrying my suitcase toward the house.

I didn't follow him right away. It occurred to me that I had no idea where I was or how far it was to the nearest neighbor or anywhere else, for that matter. I was in the middle of nowhere. In a place I knew next to nothing about. And it was getting dark. My cell phone had zero bars. Even if I could get reception, who would I call?

I sat on a well-worn leather couch in Jack's living room, trying to think of something pleasant to say to his daughter. Anna's caregiver had parked her in her wheelchair so that she was facing me. She wasn't exactly facing me. Facing me implied eye contact. Anna had a slack expression on her face and appeared to be staring off into space. I watched a string of drool trickle from the corner of her mouth and dangle precariously over the arm of her chair. I entertained myself by placing bets on how long it would take for a puddle to form on the carpet.

Jack was in the other room talking with the caregiver about medication schedules, when Anna was last fed, if she needed a bath, and then he told her he wouldn't need her to come back until the following week. My understanding of how much care Anna required was based solely on what

Jack shared with me when he was feeling overwhelmed. If caring for her was so overwhelming, then why would he ask the caregiver to stay away for so long while he had a house guest? Wouldn't it make more sense to have an extra set of hands so that he could spend more quality time with me? Was I being selfish?

Then it hit me. He expected me to help with Anna's care while I was there. I didn't sign up for that. That was one of the reasons I wanted to stay at the hotel. I didn't know how comfortable I'd be staying at his house after meeting him in person for the first time. A hotel room provided a safety net in case things didn't work out the way I'd hoped. Now I was stuck in Jack's house without another option.

The front door shutting with a heavy thud pulled me out of my thoughts.

"Right. How are you and Anna getting on, then?" Jack beamed at me like he couldn't imagine a happier scenario.

"I'm not used to being around children," I said. "I'm not sure what to talk to her about."

He laughed. It was an unsettling sound, given the circumstances. What could possibly be funny at that moment?

"You have more in common than you realize," he said.

What the fuck was that supposed to mean? How could I possibly have anything in common with a drooling eight-year-old in a wheelchair? Whoa. That was insensitive. Just plain mean, really.

Something made me look at her. Maybe it was my guilt. I don't know. But when I looked at her, I swear she was making eye contact. That spaciness was gone. So was the slackness of her expression. She looked agitated. Afraid almost. Her eyes moved back and forth in her head wildly, like she was trying to show me something. Tell me something.

How long had it been since I'd eaten anything? Four hours? Five? I was starting to get hangry, and possibly hallucinating. I was directing my anger toward Anna. At least I was having some very unkind thoughts about her. None of this was her fault. That I knew for sure. At the moment, it felt like the only thing I was sure of. Had she been trying to communicate with me?

"I think I need to eat something. I'm feeling a little weird," I said.

"I cooked a roast yesterday; I'll fix us some sandwiches," he said.

The sandwich was delicious and took the edge off my hanger. That feeling was short-lived, though, because soon after we ate it was time to feed Anna.

Anna ate everything through a feeding tube, and the conditions had to be just right for her to be able to eat and safely digest her food. If she got overexcited or laughed too hard, she was in danger of throwing up, which also meant that she was in danger of choking to death on her vomit.

I did the dishes and cleaned up the kitchen, so I wouldn't have to be in the room when Jack fed her. I'd heard too many horror stories about how often she'd almost asphyxiated because she aspirated her own vomit while eating. So often, in fact, that it seemed strange to me how many times she'd beaten the odds.

By the time Jack had finished feeding Anna, changing her diaper, bathing her, and putting her to bed, I was ready for a stiff drink. Sadly, Jack didn't keep alcohol in the house. He told me he'd stopped drinking in case he needed to wake up in the middle of the night to rush Anna to the hospital. Apparently, it happened often enough that he gave up drinking, except occasionally. In moderation.

The loud ticking of the clock in the kitchen kept time with my mounting anxiety. I needed a drink. Something to calm my nerves. Something to relax me. Especially if Jack planned on getting naked with me that evening. This setting wasn't exactly ideal for a first-time romantic encounter. If he didn't have something in the house to alter my current state of mind, it was going to take hours of foreplay to get me in the right mood. First-time jitters coupled with my fears of something happening to Anna while we were having sex made my anxiety ratchet up another notch. Each time I pictured myself in bed with Jack, my brain would replace the fantasy with an image of the sister with spinal meningitis in the original version of Stephen King's *Pet Sematary*. The book is terrifying enough, but that movie, that character was permanently burned into my psyche. And my fucked-up psyche was creating a comparison between Zelda dying alone and my fears of Anna dying in the next room while we had sex. If she died while I was there, I'd blame myself. Jack would probably blame me too. But it was his fault I was at the house. I hadn't asked to stay there. I was perfectly happy staying at the hotel.

Sometime after midnight, I found myself naked, aroused, and chemically altered. Jack had a stash of hash brownies in the freezer. He'd given up alcohol but not the need to disassociate from the realities in his very stressful life. I wanted to eat a whole brownie by myself, but he cautioned me about their potency, and we split one instead. I was reclining on the couch, laughing hysterically because Jack kept saying the filthiest things to me each time he lifted his head from between my thighs. Plus, laughter was sort of a nervous tic for me. Every time I found myself alone with a man for the first or second time, my anxiety eked out of me in nervous, hysterical laughter. Some men thought I was insane, and I never saw them again, but others liked the fact that I was having such a good time. If you can't laugh while having sex, you're with the wrong partner. Granted, Jack's beard tickled the insides of my thighs, and the hash was definitely responsible for some of my giggles, too. And the closer I got to reaching climax, the less nervous I felt.

"I want to fuck you," he said.

There was roughness to his voice, a certain tone I'd

come to recognize as a sign of desire. He wanted me. That sound in his voice was almost enough to push me over the edge. "Yes."

That one word was enough of an invitation. He was inside me before I could second-guess myself. I should have asked him to wear a condom. Too late. He felt so good.

Until he didn't.

There was a sharp, stabbing pain inside my uterus. Each time he thrust into me, the pain intensified. Each time the pain sharpened, his thrusts became more erratic. More forceful.

"Stop." My voice was barely a whisper.

His grip on my hips tightened. The motion of his hips and pelvis increased.

"Stop." My voice, like my body, was growing weaker.

He didn't stop. No matter how much I begged.

He fucked me into silence. Until I could barely catch my breath. Until I lost consciousness.

I woke to the sound of an alarm going off. Anna's oxygen monitor. I tried to sit up. I couldn't. I was alone on the couch. I could hear Jack talking to Anna in the next room, but I couldn't make out what he was saying. The alarm kept going off. A loud, repetitive screeching that reminded me of a woman screaming. And then it stopped.

The silence was worse than the alarm.

Several moments passed. I lay there, barely able to move. Nauseated. Head pounding. Vision blurred. Still naked.

Jack stepped into the living room. "She won't be bothering us anymore."

Was Anna dead? Had he killed her?

"Ah-nah," I said, slurring my words.

"Don't try to speak. Save your energy."

He sat down on the other end of the couch and ran his hand down my calf. I tried to move away from him but couldn't. All I could do was shift slightly onto my side but couldn't move my legs. They felt like they were glued together. Something sticky, viscous, oozed from between my thighs. My period wasn't due, but the cramping in my lower back and abdomen made me second-guess my intimate knowledge of my own body.

When he pried my legs apart, more ooze poured out. It smelled like rotting garbage and something more disgusting. He climbed on top of me. I didn't have the strength to fight him. I managed to turn my head enough not to choke on my vomit when I threw up. The pain was much worse. By some miracle of my failing anatomy, I blacked out sooner this time.

I remained on that couch for three days and three nights. Each time I woke up, he violated me. Pouring more of his poison into me. My body grew weaker. My thoughts more scattered. By the third night, I couldn't remember my name. Couldn't feel his body slithering over mine. The pain was finally gone. So was my will to live.

On the fourth day, I woke up in a wheelchair. Anna's wheelchair. There was a feeding tube shoved down my throat. My thoughts were clear again. I knew where I was. Knew my name. Knew I was wearing a diaper. That I had soiled myself. I was aware of everything happening around me, but I couldn't move or speak. I couldn't scream. I couldn't run. I couldn't fight. Fear is a useless emotion when you can't do anything to alleviate it.

I had always been careful when having sex. I used birth control. Condoms. Got tested regularly. Paid attention to my cycle religiously. Only once did I make a mistake. I'd accidentally skipped a pill or two while I had the flu in college and got careless after a night of drinking. I had an abortion. Not just because I couldn't remember the name of the guy I'd slept with, but also because I was a sophomore in college and didn't plan on dropping out of school to become a mom. After that, I asked my gynecologist for a tubal ligation. He refused. Said I was too young to make a decision like that. Said I just hadn't met the right man yet. Someday I'd want children.

I never wanted children. Had no desire to become a mother. No innate urge to nurture a child. Now I was becoming a child. Or, at least, my body was changing into something that resembled a child. A sick, nonverbal, drooling child confined to a wheelchair.

Jack was right. I did have more in common with Anna than I thought. He'd never had a daughter. Anna had been one of his victims. How long had she been trapped in that house with that monster? Or whatever the hell he was. Man. Monster. What difference did it make now? Like her, I was trapped in his house. Trapped inside my body. Wasting away. Waiting for death. A death that would only come when he decided it was time. When he grew tired of feeding me. Bathing me. Changing my diapers. When he brought the next woman home to replace me.

SÉANCE FOR A LOVER

By Marge Simon

His father threatens to cut him off.
Not the first time, won't be the last.
The opiates are delivered by
a mincing little man with oily hair.

He dreams the woman, calls her Sugar,
hair coiled in serpentine braids
which she allows him to unwind
in auburn strands upon the pillow.

She serves him tea and powdered scones.
Tired, mindless but for his pleasure,
he pushes it aside, beds her in a sad room
smelling of sex and stale perfume.

Later, they talk of Coleridge and Byron,
of graves beneath the sea, moon-bathed lovers.
He fancies there is a trace of sand on her lips,
only a fingertip away, but she withdraws,
he may not touch her face.

There is no one else in the house.
Paper birds torn from love letters
flap to the floor from another time,
stark on the long brown carpet.

Her abortion went well, considering
the unwashed tools, deep garnet stained.
She stumbles out the door,
lines the cobblestones with blood,
home to the street of red lights.

Cold chains the winter night.
It was a dream, he tells himself,
closing the damask curtains.
He reaches for comfort, strikes a match,
only to discover the pipe is empty.

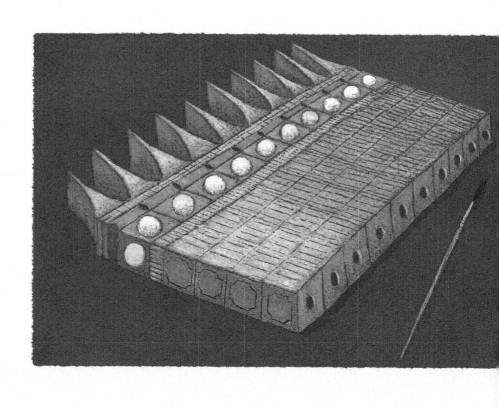

DUST TO DUST

By Rebecca Rowland

Connecticut, March 1925

"Charles, you know we have that dinner with the Newburys on Saturday." Julia examined her hair, a cleanly curled bob circling her head, its sharp angles forcing the eye to draw an imaginary line that extended beneath her cheekbones and across her small, pursed mouth. The prodigious mirror in the hallway was the best place for her to check her reflection, as the natural light streaming from the front door was bright enough to catch any stray hairs or smudges of makeup but not severe enough to make her feel self-conscious of the ever-growing cracks and crazes along an otherwise immaculate complexion.

"Mmm." Her husband's curt acknowledgment of her reminder punctuated the conversation like a muffled fart. His eyes darted upward, over the edge of his newspaper and toward the slice of hallway visible from his seat at the head of the dining room table. The early morning sunlight radiated from the wide mirror, making the area appear to glow.

"What time is Mr. Clark expecting you?" Julia turned and stood in the doorway, her body a jarring eclipse blocking out much of the light.

Charles glanced at the clock on the mantel, carefully folded the newspaper in half, and placed it gingerly aside. "I suppose I should be heading out," he said. His knees made a soft snapping sound as he rose to standing.

Julia patted the side of his arm as he walked toward the hall coat rack. "Good luck on your first day, Charles," she said, her voice light but distracted.

"It's only a consultation position," he replied, but she had already disappeared behind the swinging door of the kitchen, leaving Charles to gather his briefcase and hat alone. He stopped only momentarily to check his reflection in the mirror before heading out the door.

The Waterbury Clock Company complex sprawled across nearly a full block of Cherry Street. Dorothy Kelly stood on the sidewalk just opposite the front door, hesitant. A warm hand grabbed hold of her elbow from behind.

"You made it!" Alice slid her hand under Dorothy's arm, hooking it with her own and pulling her close. "I'm so glad."

Dorothy smiled and looked at the ground. "I can't thank you enough for getting me the job," she said. "After what happened at the bank, I..." Her voice faded softly away as her head dipped even lower, tucking the end of the statement somewhere safe inside her coat.

"Don't be silly," said Alice brightly. "You'll be so much happier here. The fringe benefits alone—" Alice punctuated the end of this exclamation with a dramatic sweep of her arm. "Just wait until tonight."

Dorothy lifted her face. "Tonight?"

Alice winked. "You'll see." She tugged at her friend's arm. "Now, come on; I'll introduce you to Dodds."

The third floor of the industrial building featured large warehouse-sized rooms packed with seemingly endless rows of long wooden tables and chairs. Windows stretching to the ceiling comprised nearly the entire back wall, and at each table, two or three girls, each about Dorothy's age, bent forward over their tasks, shiny queues of palm-sized Baby Ben clocks arranged neatly in front of them. Mrs. Dodds, the supervisor, a woman of forty buttoned tightly into a high-necked blouse, led Dorothy around the factory floor.

"You will be paid eight cents a dial," she explained curtly. "Not by the hour, so it's best to use your time wisely. However, you must be meticulous. Any clock with imprecise numbers will count as a loss, and its cost will be deducted from your week's pay." She stopped short at a table with an empty chair. "This will be your seat. Each morning, leave your personals in the locker, then collect your supplies. You'll be given a set daily allotment of radium powder to mix with the water to make the paint. Be sure not to waste it." She gestured for Dorothy to sit. "Do you have any questions?"

Dorothy slid into the chair and shook her head, placing the tray of items on the space of tabletop in front of her. She picked up the slim paintbrush and touched the camel hair tip with her finger.

"And take care to keep the brush tip pointed. A sloppy brush is certain to smear your work." With this last statement, Mrs. Dodds turned sharply away and walked toward the front of the room, her eyes scanning the women working with keen attentiveness.

"I'm Louise." The girl sitting next to her leaned her small blonde head toward Dorothy. "Did she show you how to dip?" Louise made a small "o" in the air with her paintbrush.

"Oh, uh...yes," Dorothy stammered. She unscrewed the tiny jar of paint and dipped her brush daintily inside, wiping the sides of the tip on the inside of the jar's mouth.

Louise laughed gaily. "No, you'll waste too much paint that way. Plus, it dries so quickly. You'll have to wet it again, anyway, and they don't like waste." She glanced quickly around, then continued. "A few months back, they told us to stop using our mouths. They told us to dip the brush in water to remoisten it. But after a week or so, there was so much loss—radium on the water bowl—that they told us just to go back to whatever had been working before.

Personally, I think it was much ado about nothing. It's so much easier this way. See? Like this." She placed the tip of the brush in her mouth, then pulled it from her closed lips to narrow the camel hairs into a sharp point. Then, she dipped the tip nimbly into the paint and drew a six on the clock face she held in her hand. "Lip, dip, paint."

"Mrs. Dodds said not to put the brush in my mouth," Dorothy said. "She was pretty insistent about that."

"Nonsense," said Louise, wetting the brush with her mouth again. "It's the only way to get it right. Someone started spreading a rumor that licking the brush was what killed Frances, that's all." She nodded at Dorothy as she tapped the brush into her jar of paint. "That's whose seat you got, er, uh..."

"Dorothy—Dottie."

"Ah, you're Alice's pal, yeah? She mentioned you'd be coming."

Dorothy nervously arranged her supplies in what seemed like the most logical order for her task.

Louise leaned toward her again and lowered her voice. "We're all headed to a speakeasy in New Haven after work. You have to join us—you simply must. And leave a little paint in your mixing jar." She winked, then returned to concentrating on her work.

Dorothy looked pensively at the brush in her hand, then slowly raised it to her mouth and felt the hairs roll together into a point along her tongue. The paint residue didn't taste bad: no worse than ordinary craft glue, and she tapped the brush into the jar just as Louise had done, then carefully outlined the number one on her first clock dial.

The women were settling back down into their workstations after lunch when the tightly buttoned supervisor noisily cleared her throat and called for their attention. Two men in expensive-looking suits stood to her left;

Dorothy recognized the shorter one as the man who had hired her days earlier.

"That's Mr. Clark," whispered Louise, reading her mind. "He never comes down to the floor unless it's something big." She squinted at the taller man. "I've never seen *him* before."

"Ladies." Mr. Clark's voice was surprisingly deep and low for a man of such slight stature. "I want to introduce you to Dr. Charles Flynn." He pointed at his companion, who nodded at the crowd in a gentlemanly greeting. "Dr. Flynn has joined Waterbury Clock as its chief medical consultant."

Mr. Clark swallowed hard before continuing. "Our dial painters are very precious to us. Waterbury is a family. Of the many applicants petitioning for your jobs, we selected *you*, and we want to ensure *you* receive the best treatment possible." He paused a moment and scanned the crowd of women, hundreds of expectant eyes glued to his every motion. "Waterbury's gals come first, just as you have placed, and continue to place, Waterbury first.

"Should any of you have a concern—a bit of a cold coming on, irritable skin, even a minor headache that won't abate—you needn't take off work to visit the physician's office—or trouble yourself with the worry of paying for that visit. Dr. Flynn is here to address all of your needs and answer any questions you might have, completely free of charge."

With this, Dr. Flynn stepped forward and cleared his throat, appearing to want to clarify what the manager had advised, but Mr. Clark held his arm slightly aloft, a traffic cop holding a rogue commuter at bay. "Thank you for your attention. We'll let you continue with your work."

A few feet away, Mrs. Dodds played nervously with the top button of her blouse, her fingers drumming a tiny march along the thin ruffle trim that encircled her throat as Mr. Clark wrapped up his short declaration. Dorothy looked from the supervisor to Dr. Flynn, who was now frowning slightly. Mr. Clark tipped his head, and the two men walked past Mrs. Dodds without acknowledgment and disappeared through the exit.

Like the other women around her, Louise resumed her painting. Dorothy looked again at the tightly buttoned woman; she had dropped her hands from her neck and was gazing absent-mindedly at the doorway where the men had absconded. Then she smoothed the waist of her skirt with both palms and walked briskly back to her desk.

In the supply room, as the other women stood in line to hand in their equipment before leaving for the evening, Alice tipped her head to peer into Dorothy's paint-mixing jar. "You still have a bit left," she whispered, then wrapped her arm under her friend's. "Come with me. I have something marvelous to show you."

They stepped out of the Friday evening bustle and slipped into a nearby lavatory. Inside, Louise and a woman she'd been introduced to as Katherine stood facing one another in front of a wide ceramic sink, brandishing their dial painting brushes like conductor batons. Louise was carefully painting the seashell buttons along Katherine's blouse; Katherine was outlining Louise's lips.

The latter turned quickly to the sound of the door opening and shooed at Dorothy and Alice with her free hand. "Shut the door, quick!" she whispered loudly.

Alice did as she was told but walked nonchalantly toward the others. "Aw, Dobbs doesn't mind. She's the one who suggested this last year, remember?"

Louise made a duck face with her lips as Katherine pulled her brush away. "That's if she doesn't see it," Louise said. "There's a big difference between *thinking* the company stock is being used for novelty and *knowing* it. Plausible deniability."

Dorothy inched closer. "What are you doing?" she asked curiously.

Louise winked at her. "Remember when I told you to hold onto any leftover paint? This is why." She pointed to her mouth and then to Katherine's blouse, indicating the freshly painted line of buttons parading from her clavicle to her waist. "Just wait until the moon is up."

Dorothy thought for a moment. "Should be pretty soon. Sun still sets early in January."

"Do you mind if I use some of your leftover?" Alice asked, nodding toward the jar in Dorothy's hand. "I used all of mine up today, I'm afraid."

"Gunning for a top producer bonus, are we?" Katherine said, raising an eyebrow and smiling.

Dorothy surrendered her jar, and Alice accepted it and dipped her brush inside. "Someone's got to be the cat's meow, doll," she said, leaning down to catch her reflection in the chrome faucet and smiling widely. She removed her brush and began to painstakingly paint each tooth surface. "I like the idea of a boy in uniform gazing down at my work glowing beside him as he lies on his bunk at night," she said, her words slightly squishy as she kept her jaw rigid.

Dorothy leaned on a nearby stool. "Are you sure this is okay?"

"*Not to worry,*" Louise screwed her voice into a pantomime of Mr. Clark's. "*If you swallow any radium, it'll make your cheeks rosy.*" The other two women laughed. "In all seriousness," Louise continued, "it's quite healthy. Why do you think it's in all those tonics and face creams and toothpastes nowadays?"

"All the doctors are touting its miracle cures," added Katherine. She motioned for Louise to turn her head, then dipped her brush into the mixing jar and scraped the last vestiges of paint onto her brush. "Are you sure this is what you want?" she asked Louise. "It might be a little off-putting."

Louise ran her hand through the curls at the bottom of her hair and smiled wickedly. "I feel like looking dangerous tonight. Doesn't everyone sometimes?"

"All right," said Katherine, and she held her arm steady as she drew lines along Louise's cheekbones and along the top of her collarbone.

"Ladies?" The voice of Mrs. Dobbs through the door see-sawed between sing-songy and stern. "Let's go. We're all anxious to get moving for the weekend."

Dorothy was the last of the four to turn in her materials and grab her coat from the locker area. When she finally stepped into the early evening chill, the sky was as black as it would be at midnight. Alice, Katherine, and Louise sat huddled together in the back seat of the waiting blue Durant Star F-25 at the curb, Louise's boyfriend Aldore at the wheel. Louise pressed her face against the window and smiled when she saw her tablemate emerge, but as she did, Dorothy felt her stomach drop sickly into the bowels of her pelvis. For a moment, it wasn't Louise who grinned at her but a terrifying Jack-o-Lantern. In the dim light, an eerie skeletal head of arched eyebrows, angular cheekbones, and grimacing lips glowed menacingly from behind the glass.

Dorothy did not continue toward the car until the rear door opened and Louise spilled from its contents. "I'll hop in the front," she called. "There's plenty of room."

As she slid onto the seat next to Alice, Dorothy finally understood what the girls had done. In the gloaming of the interior, Katherine's buttons and fingernails were alight with greenish illumination; Alice smiled conspiratorially, and her teeth glowed so brightly, they shone like tiny night-lights through the pale skin of her upper lip. Alice began to laugh, the luminescence in her open mouth zig-zagging like a bucket of fireflies when she shook her head. "You didn't brush yourself off?" she asked.

"Brush myself off?" Dorothy echoed.

Louise leaned over the seat and handed her a compact. "There's so much radium dust in the air. They tell us not to leave without a proper fluff to recover the excess. The waste of material alone..." She pointed to the mirror. "Take a look for yourself, doll."

Dorothy held the small round mirror in front of her face and gasped. Sure enough, her hair, her delicate porcelain skin, even her fingers radiated with a slightly greenish incandescence. "I look like some kind of...specter," she said at last and closed the compact with a quick snap.

Alice hooked her arm under Dorothy's as she had that morning and leaned close. "You're officially one of the ghost girls now, Dottie," she said. Dorothy said nothing back, only stared at her apparitional reflection in the window's glass as the car drove through the night, headed downtown.

Hours later, Aldore's car slowed to a stop outside of the ladies' boarding house where Dorothy shared a room. Alice teetered sideways toward her, partially out of affection, but mostly from the covert cocktails they'd imbibed in the basement hideaway below Pete's Pizzeria. She leaned her head into the crook of Dorothy's neck and sighed happily. "I'm so glad you came, Dottie," she said, then squeezed her friend's arm lightly.

Dorothy smiled and patted Alice's head. "Make sure to drink a tall glass of water before you lie down," she said motherly, then opened the car door and stretched her legs outside. She thanked Aldore and wished the women a good weekend, then hurried toward the building's entrance. Mrs. Murphy, the residence's proprietor, did not take kindly to her tenants traipsing about in the middle of the night, so Dorothy was extra cautious as she eased the door shut behind her and tip-toed up the stairs to the room at the end of the hall.

Mary Ann was still awake, sitting in her twin bed, a frayed copy of Modern Woman magazine open on her lap. She pushed the reading to the side when Dorothy entered and glanced at the clock on the table between their beds. "Goodness. I was wondering what happened to you." Mary Ann said, pushing the covers off her legs. "You'd think a gal with a new job at a clock company would know how to tell time."

Dorothy unzipped her dress and stepped carefully out of it, then began unhooking her stockings. "I'm so sorry. The girls invited me to go out for a bit after. I should have come home first to tell you." She glanced at her reflection in the mirror and touched her cheek. "I'm too tired to wash." She yawned.

Mary Ann shuffled over on her sheets, lay down on her side, and patted the open area in front of her torso. "I don't mind. I'm stripping the bed tomorrow anyway." Dorothy turned off the lamp, slid into the space where her girlfriend's hand had been just moments before, and rested her head on the pillow. Mary Ann's hand softly caressed her face in the dim light. "Still made up, like my own private Georgia Hale," she murmured.

Dorothy reached up and kissed Mary Ann long and hard on the mouth.

When Dorothy returned her head to the pillow, Mary Ann squinted and traced a finger along her cheekbone. "You're glowing," she said. "I guess the rumors are true—radium really is magical. Like star dust."

January 1926

"All I'm saying is that there is no need to draw unnecessary attention." Mr. Clark stared unblinkingly at Dr. Flynn, who shifted uncomfortably in his desk chair. "Paying compensation for damaged laundry is one thing; getting these women all riled up over a bit of aches and pains is quite another."

Charles Flynn tapped his fountain pen on the desk blotter. "Damaged laundry?"

Mr. Clark ran his hand through his hair. "Oh, a neighbor complained that the fumes from the factory discolored her sheets. Next thing you know, the company is issuing five-dollar checks for replacements. Trouble is, once one woman lodges a grievance, suddenly the whole block shows up with their hands out."

"Like the mother with the shoes?" Charles turned his head to look out of the nearby window. Dishwater clouds covered the already graying sky, blanketing the view in a perpetual dusk. Charles's eyes landed on a schoolyard in the distance, a thin coating of ice slicking its blacktop. A faded blue tarp covered a small framed area alongside it. *A sandbox, likely,* thought Charles. *Where the boy with the brown shoes that turned white had played.*

Mr. Clark frowned at him. "I hired you to reassure our employees that radium is nothing to worry about. It's going to be in supplements next year, for Christ's sake."

Charles watched the man's countenance in the window's reflection, then exhaled audibly. "Speaking of which, my four o'clock should be arriving soon." He turned to shuffle the papers on his desk until his fingers landed on a small square of paper with a note. "Pyorrhea, perhaps... some kind of ache in her jaw, she says." He shrugged. "I'm not a dentist, but I'll—"

"Try to resolve it here, please," Mr. Clark interrupted. "Last year, a specialist came by, inquiring about the ingredients in the paint. Apparently, phossy jaw is making the rounds."

"You use phosphorus?"

"Not a bit," Mr. Clark said, "and I told him that. But he said he'd been seeing a few cases in the area that resembled it, wanted to track down the factory that might be the root." He rested his hat on Charles's desk, purposefully covering the appointment note. "I was under the impression that your role here at Waterbury was crystal clear, Dr. Flynn."

Charles cleared his throat. "I am simply...I'm not a physician. I'm an industrial toxicologist." He paused and lowered his voice. "I'm slightly uncomfortable that the women have been led to believe otherwise."

Mr. Clark stared at Charles until the doctor looked away. "Waterbury is committed to maintaining its fine reputation producing quality materials for our nation's soldiers. Part of that commitment is ensuring its work continues unimpeded by misinformation and frivolity. If there's some confusion about our expectations of you, Dr. Flynn, we can certainly revisit the terms under which you were hired."

The two men said nothing for a long moment until a soft rap on the door punctuated the silence. Mr. Clark placed his fedora on his head and nodded to Charles before turning the knob. "Well, hello, ladies," he said in a booming voice upon seeing the two women standing in the entrance. "You two have a pleasant afternoon," he added, then shifted around Alice and Dorothy and disappeared down the hallway.

Charles invited the women inside. "You can leave your coats there," he said, pointing to a rack by the door. "Please, sit down."

Alice removed her coat and handed it to Dorothy, who folded it gingerly over her arm. "Thank you for seeing me," Alice said. "My name is Alice Warren, and this is my friend Dorothy Kelly." She walked with pained exertion over to the tall chairs in the corner of the office, hesitated for a moment, then climbed into one and rested her hand on her jaw.

"Alice. Dorothy." Charles nodded at each of the women, his eyes lingering on the second. She was a striking brunette with wide blue eyes and skin the color of fresh milk. Even muffled under a heavy winter coat, the curve of her waist into generous hip transfixed his gaze. The voluptuous escort seemed to sense his interest and kept her eyes centered on her friend, refusing to give him the satisfaction of an acknowledgment.

"Doctor Flynn," Alice said, her voice gravelly. "I've been to a dentist. He diagnosed me with gum disease, he said from poor nutrition. I've been extra careful in what I eat, but the pain in my mouth just keeps getting worse." She rubbed the side of her face and winced. "I've had three teeth removed, and a few others are beginning to feel loose."

Charles switched on the overhead lamp and placed his hand on the back of Alice's neck. "Tip your head back for me, please, and open your mouth. Let's have a look."

Alice did as she was told, and Charles had to steady himself to keep from flinching at the putrid stench that emanated from the woman's open mouth. It smelled like a rotting carcass, discarded drippings from a butcher shop gone rancid. He forced himself to breathe only through the small slit where his lips parted and leaned closer for a better look. The woman's gums were not just red and raw; they were nearly black in some places. Tarry. Yellowish pustules dotted the spaces where molars had once resided; a fat blister oozed puss into the empty socket below it.

Charles let go of Alice's neck and backed away slightly. "Give me a moment," he said, keeping his voice as even as he could muster. He opened a nearby drawer and pulled out a pair of new surgical gloves. He glanced at the window, attempting to steal another look at the patient's friend but discovered with a start that she was already looking at him blankly in the reflection. He tried to cover his surprise by taking a deep breath of air, then returned to his patient. "When did you last see the dentist?" He tried to sound nonchalant, gently opening Alice's mouth with one hand and sticking a gloved index finger from another inside.

Alice's eyes shifted nervously to her friend.

"I went with her last month, just before Christmas," Dorothy said.

His gaze stayed fixed on the inside of Alice's mouth. "Have you taken anything for the pain?" He poked at a nearby incisor. It wiggled slightly, and Alice winced and audibly sucked in a breath.

"Just aspirin," Dorothy responded.

"What's causing this?" Alice blinked back tears.

Charles removed his hands and turned his head in grateful reprieve from the fetor. He faced the window again, resting his gaze on the covered sandbox, Mr. Clark's staunch instructions—and unequivocal threat—reverberating in his mind. In the mirror of window glass, the woman's friend stared at him again, her large, bright eyes burning holes into him. He met them for a brief moment, then turned back toward Alice. "I'm not usually in the business of telling young women such things, but I assume...you're not married, correct?"

Alice frowned in confusion but shook her head slowly. "No," she whispered.

Charles leaned backward against a nearby table. "Unfortunately, particularly following some of the reform movements of the past decade, there seems to be a rise in what I can only categorize as, well, the wobbling of the country's moral compass, you might say."

Alice's eyes darted quickly from Charles to Dorothy and back, trying to decipher the doctor's meaning.

Charles crossed his arms and uttered a heavy sigh. "My strongest inclination is that you've developed an unfortunate progression of Cupid's disease."

"Cupid's—?" Alice began to echo his statement and stopped. Her face reddened. "I...I..."

"Syphilis?" Dorothy said, suddenly understanding. "But she—"

Charles rearranged his arms across his chest and raised his voice slightly. "I can certainly draw some blood, send for a test to confirm it, but—"

"No." Alice slid from the chair, her face burning. "No, thank you, Doctor Flynn." She kept her eyes fixed on the ground but reached out toward her friend to take back her overcoat. Dorothy helped her put it back on and kept her arm wrapped around her friend's shoulders as the two walked toward the door.

"I don't understand." Mary Ann sat on the edge of her bed, running a silver brush through her hair that made shushing noises as Dorothy recounted the afternoon's event to her. "Why didn't she stay and get the test?"

Dorothy sat down next to her and lowered her voice to nearly a whisper. "V.D.? You think Alice wants her family knowing, *anyone* knowing she has venereal disease?" She pulled her legs onto the bed and crossed them into a pretzel. "Louise is gone. She and Aldore got married over the summer. Alice wants to find a husband more than anything in the world, and now, with this..." Dorothy sighed and looked down at her hands. "She's taking a leave from the factory. Her parents are sending her to a sanatorium. They're telling people it's phossy jaw."

Mary Ann put down her brush and placed her hand on Dorothy's shoulder. "Maybe it's time you did the same. Took a leave."

Dorothy shrugged her hand away. "Are you joking? I am the fastest painter on the floor now." She lifted her head proudly. "I can complete 250 watches in one day sometimes." She took Mary Ann's hand in hers. "This is what we talked about. We don't need husbands to support us. We can build our own lives."

Mary Ann squeezed her hand and smiled. "I'm just tired of seeing the love of my life glow like quinine under the sheets. It's not natural, Dottie. And I don't care what they are saying—something isn't right about this."

"We'll see," said Dorothy, jumping up from the bed. She must have pinched a nerve when she did so, she thought, and rubbed the back of her waist with one hand. Her spine was starting to throb.

March 1927

Hoagy Carmichael crooned from the record player in the common room, where a number of the residents sat on sofas, sewing and knitting while they listened to the music on the lazy Saturday afternoon. Mrs. Murphy entered from the kitchen and asked for a volunteer to walk to the bakery; she'd forgotten to pick up bread for that evening's dinner.

It had rained frozen drizzle most of the week, but the day was clear and sunny, and Dorothy jumped at the excuse to move about in the fresh air. Mary Ann was in Chicago for the week visiting her family, and the pain in Dorothy's back roared full force. Without her partner to rub liniment along her spine, it was nearly intolerable. Moving eased the ache slightly, and a bit of exercise might make sleeping easier as well.

It wasn't until she had reached the sidewalk that Dorothy recognized the woman standing at the curb, the blue Durant Star F-25 idling behind her. Louise looked thin—gaunt, even—in her pale pink dress and coat, her head and neck loosely wrapped in a large scarf, although the temperature didn't seem to warrant it. "Dottie!" she called out, the smile on her face incongruous to the sickly pallor of her skin.

Dorothy carefully embraced her friend, then pulled away, keeping her hands on Louise's arms. "It's so good to see you, Louise. What's it been? A year and a half? How are you?"

Louise glanced at the car. Inside, Aldore was sitting motionless at the wheel, staring blankly out the window in the other direction. "I was hoping to catch you." She paused and cleared her throat. "I don't know if you've heard, but there is a group of dial painters in New Jersey. They are suing their employer."

Dorothy dropped her hands. "Suing? Why?" Even as she heard herself ask the question, she already knew the answer.

Louise blinked rapidly and rubbed her eyes. She cleared her throat again and continued. "They are sick. Like Frances. And Alice. Alice..."

Dorothy focused on keeping her arms steady, commanding her legs not to melt into the ground below as Louise told her the story. A few days after Alice checked into the hospital, a dentist examined her mouth again. As he prodded one of the infected sockets, the bone had simply broken under his fingers, and to everyone's horror, when he pulled his hand from her mouth, a large section of her jaw absconded with it.

"They thought it might be a blessing that perhaps all of the dead tissue had been removed, and her mouth could finally heal," Louise said. "But the infection had spread." It crept down her throat, eating away at her jugular vein until one day the nurse came to check on her, and Alice's mouth had filled with blood: thick gobs of it, spilling uncontrollably from between her lips, covering her chest in a thick, sticky blanket smelling of pennies.

Louise reached out suddenly and clutched Dorothy's arm. "It's the paint. It has to be. You aren't still working there, are you?"

Dorothy swallowed hard. "Yes, Louise. I—"

"You have to quit, Dottie. Before it's too late." Louise glanced quickly around, then carefully unhooked the end of her scarf from the knot at her neck and slowly unwrapped it. Dorothy gasped before she could stop herself. Just below Louise's cornsilk hair, beneath her chin, a large round mass protruded from the side of her once slim neck. Larger than a fist, perhaps six or seven inches across, the bulbous mound stretched under her skin, tearing so many angry, dark purple welts that it nearly resembled an oversized plum swollen with rotten pulp. Louise swallowed nervously, but the enormous pustule remained firmly rooted in place as the wave passed alongside it down her throat.

Louise dropped her hand. "I went to see Dr. Flynn. Even though I didn't work for the company anymore, I thought maybe..." She turned her head, then shook it slightly. "He said it was an infected cyst from a buildup of bacteria. He told me I needed to wash better." She crossed her arms over her chest and sniffed. "To *wash better*," she repeated.

"I'm so sorry, Louise," Dorothy said finally.

"Yes, well...ghost girls, right?" Louise wrapped the scarf loosely around her neck but left her blonde waves loose. A gust of wind rushed over them, sending her tendrils aloft, swirling around her face like a Gorgon's.

Dorothy tightly clutched the buttons along the front of her coat, but the sudden chill in the air darted between the seams and made her shiver. The sharp pain in her back intensified, and she held her breath, hoping to quell the anguish.

Louise reached out and touched Dorothy's arm, and before her friend could respond, forced a smile before turning around and climbing back into the car.

"Ghost girls," Dorothy whispered. She watched in silence as the blue Durant pulled slowly away from the curb and down the street. Louise's head leaned against the window glass, a hollow skull with gossamer skin, her eyes staring straight ahead, unblinking, like those of an emaciated corpse.

CHILDREN OF BOTO

By Angela Yuriko Smith

In Brazil, abortion is illegal.

This doesn't stop women from seeking it. An estimated one to four million illegal abortions occur in Brazil annually. In many cases, a pregnancy may be the result of rape or incest. In 1940, the penal codes were amended to waive punishment in those situations, but the burden of proof was on the women until recently. Still, vehement opposition from the Catholic Church and some doctors has been an obstacle.

Often, those who can least afford it are victimized the most—women who can barely feed themselves are forced to bear the punishment of sexual abuse. The maternal mortality rate is 45.8 per 100,000 live births, down from 68% in 1998. Illegal and unsafe abortion is the fourth leading cause of maternal mortality in the country.

The potential risk factors for suicide in depressed pregnant women were being single, divorced, or widowed; lower age; low education level; and low socioeconomic class.

Banning abortion isn't working.

Statistics from National Library of Medicine *and* Human Rights Watch.

Ana was weighed down in every way imaginable.

Her heart, her belly, and any future were being stretched beyond recognition with unwanted baby. She couldn't say who the father was. The alley was dark. She just remembered the smell of cachaça and sweat. She was told not to worry. No one would blame her for carrying the child of Boto.

Boto was a myth. A magical pink dolphin that emerged from the river as a beautiful man in a white suit. He attended parties under the full moon, seducing young women. Under his spell, they would spend the night in lovemaking. The woman always became pregnant after.

Ana was sure the man who attacked her was no myth. There was no lovemaking under a full moon. He was shirtless, along with being suitless. That was a story meant to excuse what happened to her and women like her. Men overcome by passion were blameless. It was women who paid for this. With fewer options to succeed, a baby, wanted or not, was extra baggage.

She looked across the water that flowed beneath her. It didn't matter if Boto was real. A handsome man in a white suit would have been better, but the result would be the same. She would be left with this child and no support. They could be hungry together. A flash of white on the water distracted her.

Below, river dolphins played carelessly in the swift current. The father of this baby was probably somewhere doing the same. There were always more women walking home late from work. There were plenty to choose from. She was replaceable. She knotted the rope around the truss.

She wished she were a dolphin. She wished she were a man. She wished she'd taken a different route home that night. Most of all, she wished she had choice. There weren't many things she could control. She would take hold of the little control that was still hers. From her perspective, the only direction left to her was down, so down she went.

The moon broke free from the clouds. The dolphins swam closer, oblivious to the woman swinging her legs over the edge and then falling, arms outstretched, to join them. She stopped just short of the water, toes nearly dipping into the waves. The dolphins watched until she was still. Bathed in lunar light, she resembled an angel descending from on high, and then the clouds returned, and with them, the darkness. She returned to being unseen.

I ENJOY BEING A GIRL

By Donna J. W. Munro

Soon...

When it came, I was in fifth grade. At least I knew it was coming because Mom wasn't as religious as most of the moms, who didn't tell their daughters anything. Everything she'd whispered to me, every nightmare detail, came true. The pains split my insides like a knife, and even though she'd told me about it, the shock from the stark red bloom in my white panties forced a gasp from me. I couldn't move, didn't know how to clean up, and sat there watching drops of blood hit the surface of the toilet water and sink like a secret.

The nurse was kind when she saw my face. I didn't even have to tell her. She handed me a pad as thick as a brick. We stuck it in place, and I wrapped my jacket around my hips to hide my stained shorts.

No one stared at me, though I couldn't understand how they didn't.

I was bleeding.

I felt like a monster.

The girl I'd been died with a grunt and a gush. Who I'd become felt alien. I wore myself like a mask the rest of the day, wondering if the kind looks I got from the teachers meant the nurse had told them. I ran home, not giving my friends a chance to ask what was wrong.

At home, Mom taught me how to wrap the pad so that no one had to look at the blood. If I used enough TP, no one would even smell what was happening.

It was secret.

Smelly.

Gross.

I cried for days behind my schoolbooks, in bathroom stalls, into my pillow. Even after the blood faded away, I knew everything was changed forever.

I wondered if any woman was ever the same after the brutality of women's biology becomes a fact in their lives? I felt like I'd died and been replaced by a complicated, messy beast that no one wanted to look at. Least of all me. Pimples and bloat and shiny skin. Everyone had to know.

And every month, the pain was worse.

In between the cycles of my body trying to wring itself out, I grew breasts earlier and bigger than every other girl at school. My body curves thickened. We all go through it. Either we lean into these crazy changes, embracing the path through puberty as an adventure, or we learn to fear ourselves.

Other ourselves.

That was me.

During my first gynecologist visit, the doctor asked if I was sexually active as he probed me. It was the first time I was aware that I was like those cutaway backline women teachers made us color in health. I'd never acknowledged the hole there. It was...just a void that issued blood each month. Something to be afraid of. And this man inserted a cool steel scapula into it without any explanation, prying me open and peering inside like it was another world in there.

"Well?" He asked as he swabbed. "Are you?"

I shivered under a paper gown with my feet up in stirrups. A tear ran down my cheek into my hair. Couldn't he tell from looking at it? Wouldn't it be stretched or ruptured if I had? Didn't it puff up red and with wet desire if a guy, any guy, touched it...You know, after you had sex. Then you were some kind of a nympho who couldn't control it down there, got possessed by it. I'd read how it happened like that so many times in church.

"No," I whispered, though I didn't think he believed me. How could he and then be so rough? It had to be a sign. Even though I'd never done things with the boys who still looked like kids even in seventh grade, didn't him asking after it mean that I would?

My body hadn't been mine for years.

When my first real boyfriend showed up at my house and I was alone, I let him touch me there.

That might have been the first time I realized that my body wasn't mine at all.

My virginity was a "gift" to give.

My body, not me, had attracted him.

Having your first boyfriend is a threshold for girls. Boyfriends proved that you were a girl people wanted, and you weren't complete without one. That feeling of otherness all girls struggle with finally made sense once I found my first. My body wasn't mine; it was his. He could use it, kiss it, touch it, claim it with a protective arm around my shoulders or a slap on the ass.

And, of course, every day was a war of inches.

Give an inch—a bit more skin, a new touch—and the boyfriend, my boyfriend, is satisfied. My body is his to explore. A continent to conquer. But don't give too many inches. You'll be an easy conquest, then. Used and dirty and not valued. And that made you a whore. A cow that gave free milk was a cow no one would buy.

I came to see my body as anything but me. A vehicle. Bait. Something I was responsible for but not ever able to fix. It was always fat or droopy or painful or bleeding.

We continued our war of inches.

I lost the war when I was fourteen.

How do you keep your boyfriend once you've given your body to him? At first, its quantity over quality.

We fucked every day. Everywhere. Everywhen. At school. In cars. In bathrooms.

I used my skin as theater, hiding inside as he pumped and spent. Hiding as the meat of me moaned and shuddered as expected. Inside, I was a bird singing. Shattering glass with my song.

When he was done, he told me he loved me.

I knew he didn't.

How could he? He didn't even know me.

I wanted to love him like some tragic princess in a Greek play. I pantomimed. We were all false heat and promises. I held onto him that way for a whole year before it happened.

I figured it out alone in my bed, lying silently inside my body after hours of rough touches in his basement and again in his car. I examined the complaints of the tender skin he'd used. I didn't usually focus there. Since it wasn't mine, I liked to pretend it didn't exist when it wasn't in use, but there was no ignoring this.

But there, in my core, I felt something moving inside. The void there, like another distant universe, thrummed inside me. I curled around the feeling, pressing into it to understand.

It slithered through my guts, wrapping around my insides, ripping into my pieces with fine hooks. Anchors tipped with barbs tipped with teeth.

Fuck it hurt.

I hissed and sobbed each time it latched. Felt like being pierced with a knitting needle. It was moving inside me, and the way it fluttered, I knew what it was. I knew, but I shrank from the thought. How long had it been in there, growing into something that wasn't me?

I wouldn't say what it was.

It dug into the void with pulsing, throbbing heat.

It felt like being eaten from the inside. Colonized.

I groaned too loud, and Mom came in to check on me. She assumed my monthly bleed had come. She tutted and brought me a heating pad and a pill. If she knew the truth, the screaming would start. All I could do was cry.

At school, they all looked at me differently. Could they smell the tiny invader in my body? They say pregnant women glow. Did I?

All I know is that, as I walked through my day, people stared. My friends were too busy to talk. Sports, dates, homework. My boyfriend sat with me, but he looked like he wanted to be anywhere else. And inside my head, it was even worse.

The thing had grown a voice.

It didn't speak whole words.

Whispers.

Between the hallway noise, the soundtrack of a video blaring in history class, and the murmuring of my classmates, I heard it. The invader was inside of my thoughts—the only place I'd ever been myself since my first blood had come. Is this what all women are? A vessel for an invader? A parasite's host?

I couldn't tell my friends, even when the thing inside me pushed and tore and dug until I whimpered. My boyfriend moved on. Found a new land to conquer. My mom was all I had left. Only her because I had to get it out of me, and she would be the one who knew how. Wouldn't she? She had to understand. The thing wasn't me, and it wasn't of me. That dark place inside me that hadn't been mine since I was a kid had spawned it.

The little whisperer muttered things that sounded like spells and sent my body into a cascade of rippling pain. It was a demon called by the conqueror. It was implanted in me against my will.

Mom didn't believe me when I told her.

"Please listen..."

"I knew you were with him too much, damn it. Why couldn't you keep your legs closed? I didn't raise you to be a whore!"

I spent most of the night in my room, screaming into my pillow so I didn't have to listen to her or the voice inside me. But I felt it. It doubled in size, and so did the sound it made on the inside. It pressed against my thoughts like a wall.

I pressed back.

My body, I told it. Mine.

And it laughed. Stretched into me further. It wouldn't leave me. I knew it.

I would never be my own. That's what I gave up when I lost my body to that void inside. I can't control it. I can't decide when I bleed or when I give myself over to creating a new life.

I can't because they took control away from us.

Later that night, Mom opened the door and sat next to me, face puffy and eyes red. She said, "I'm sorry," "It's not your fault," and "I love you no matter what." I didn't believe her. It sounded like she wanted to convince herself as much as she wanted to convince me.

"I know someone." She whispered, eyes glancing side to side like someone might be hiding in the shadows, listening. "She used to be a doctor in the old days before the change. She'll make it all go away if we want."

She squeezed me hard and pulled me close so that all I could see was her intense gaze. Eye to eye, woman to woman.

"Only if you want, though. You have to choose this and live with whatever you will feel later. Some people can't... They..."

The monster in my belly cluttered and clutched, tearing at my insides until I groaned. It couldn't be worse than this. Nothing could be.

"Yes, anything. Please, Mom."

She wrapped me in coats and scarves so thick the warmth of spring turned the coverings into a sauna. Mom dressed the same, explaining we didn't want to be seen. We drove to the city and parked our car in an alley littered with trash that stunk of rot and death.

"She's at the end. Just... stay close."

As much as the smell overwhelmed me, I couldn't help but lean into the idea of death. It was this little monster or me. It was my body or its body. At least I could choose this battle to win my body back. I felt stronger than I had since I'd first bled. More like I piloted myself along the path I was on. Weaving through the trash, I stumbled and cut myself on a rusty wire shopping cart.

It wasn't deep, but the cut throbbed with each beat of my heart. Spots of darkness swam in my eyes. I wanted to lay down and sleep and wake up as an eight-year-old running in the sun without any of this...pain. Always so much pain and blood.

"You have to keep going if you want this." Mom dabbed at the jagged cut, then pulled me up and let me lean against her for a minute to catch my breath. "You have to keep going, because this is the only place that can help you."

She pulled me along as the blood flowed down my calf. She said I had to want it enough to get past all the shit in front of us, and I did. All I wanted was to keep this feeling of being myself. Inside me, the little thing that clutched me burrowed deeper, sending knifing spasms across my muscles. I know it heard my thoughts. Maybe even felt my hate.

Why should I carry you? Why should I have to? My life or yours, I told it as I clutched my mother's hand and limped along beside her.

In the alley above me, a woman leaned out of her window, hissing. Booing. Throwing down rotted fruit.

"I know where you're going, little whore. Baby killer!"

Other heads popped out of windows, sneering. Flinging trash. Dropping rocks.

Mom and I had to cling to the wall between stumbling sprints, hiding from the assault under ledges and fire escapes. Once, it had been legal, Mom had told me. She'd warned me that these people would try to hurt us. They used to wait outside the legal clinics, but once the clinics were closed, they moved to where they knew the police wouldn't come. They set up moving headquarters in the abandoned buildings. It was always a race to get past them and their weapons, both physical and emotional. Mom said it always had been this way.

"Save the baby!"

"Dirty trash whore murderer."

"You deserve to die on that table."

"God wants you to have that child."

Mom sobbed as a rock hit me in the shoulder. It didn't hurt, but we both gasped when it hit me.

She whispered to me between tears, "We didn't mean... for it to be this way. We just... watched it all...slip away. We let it go."

"I hate being a girl."

Mom hugged me to her and nodded into my hair. "I understand. It used to be safer to be one." Then she pulled me into a final limping jog through the gauntlet of anger. Why did they hate me? Women? Why didn't they understand that I hadn't chosen this? Not really. This thing inside me took away what little control I still had.

The long alley ended in a pile of bulky trash bags built up in an arch above a recessed door. We stumbled down the steps, smeared with rot and blood, panting. Mom knocked, and a metal slat in the door slid open. Behind it, a woman with tired eyes measured us with suspicion.

Cold tension extinguished the pain as I watched her consider me. She saw the blood on my leg, the tear tracks. Could she see my fear, too? She had to let us in. I couldn't go back through the alley again. I couldn't let them hurt me anymore, not while this thing inside ate up the tiny bloom of strength.

"Please." I hoped she saw me rising behind my shadowed eyes.

"What's the word?" she asked.

Mom looked at me with tears in her eyes. "Roe. It's Roe. Please let us in."

And the door opened.

The thin gown didn't do much against the shivering. It was cold in the operating room but not cold enough to make my teeth chatter so hard.

"It's okay," Mom said. "You're scared, and that's okay."

Doc Grace touched my shoulder. "You're sure? This is what you want?"

I pressed my hands into the spot where the creature I'd made unknowingly and unwillingly curled like a cancer inside the darkness. All I could do was nod.

She led me to the table and gently helped me place my feet in the stirrups. She warmed the scapula and gently examined me. Mom held my hand as Doc Grace prepped me.

Finally, she stood and smiled. "I'm ready to go. It's going to hurt some after. You'll need to be careful about physical activity for a few weeks. Sometimes people experience some depression after. I have to ask one last time... Is this what you want?"

I nodded. "It's my choice."

Then she got started.

CRIMES AGAINST NATURE

By Lynne Schmidt

After "Your Life" by Andrea Gibson

When they tell you that you are a crime against nature,
smile and show them your teeth.
Thank them for the compliment,
for recognizing that yes, you are more powerful than
your body dictates.

Your biology does not determine the rest of your life.

They will ask,
what kind of monster doesn't love their child?
What kind of monster would view a pregnancy as a curse,
wishing for cancer during the three minutes of purgatory
where you are both pregnant and not pregnant at once?

They will never understand skin and bone as prison,
because they will never have to.

A red crab will eat its own babies
as they frantically gather around her feet.
So how can they say that you,
in all your wholeness,
are unnatural?

When they offer to pray for you,
remind them that penance is for sinners,
and you've committed no crimes here.

They will try and try to shove
their chain store top shelf grief
down your throat, and look wide-eyed
when you dare have no shame.
They will call you an abomination,
they will say you should have your tongue ripped out.

Just remind them,
you, my darling, are only just now
finding your voice.

THE BALLAD OF FAERIE GARCIA

By Sumiko Saulson

I am ever amazed by humanity's innate ability to be absolute dirt to one another, often without really trying. Granted, my father has never been the most tactful of humans. For that reason, I should not have been surprised by his crass reaction to being told about the pregnancy.

"I bet you're sorry you yeeted the titties now, huh, Jay?"

I sighed. "No. No, I am not. And I'm not even sure I am keeping it yet. By the way, Dad? You're an asshole." We were sitting in a window booth at a crowded Denny's, the sunlight streaming gently through the window and reflecting off his cheap plastic sunglasses. I cringed inwardly, wondering if anyone had heard him outing me in the middle of the restaurant?

"I've always been an asshole." Dad shrugged. "I guess that's why your mother left me."

I shook my head in silence, staring at a bird flying off in the distance to avoid making eye contact as I anxiously rocked my sneakered foot back and forth under the table. I had no intention of getting into it with him about why my mother divorced him.

Just then, our waitress arrived, efficiently distributing our plates on the table. The inviting aroma of fresh pancakes and butter rose up from the table like a soothing balm of comfort food and childhood memories.

"Here is your syrup, sir," she cheerfully announced as she set the clear glass bottle with its old-fashioned metal nozzle on the table before me.

I smiled. "Thank you, kindly." Her proper gendering of me had been very intentional, and a pleasant relief after my dad's having just gotten done bellowing about my mastectomy for the whole room to hear. She had to have heard him but appeared unfazed. I recognized her from the last time I was down here with my mother. She'd flirted with Mom a little and talked to us a bit, and I recalled she told me she was a lesbian. A card-carrying member of the Alphabet Mafia. I am so lucky that I live in the San Francisco Bay Area.

"What I don't get," Dad said loudly, "is why you aren't sure you want an abortion. I mean, if you really are a man, why would you want to carry a baby? Guys don't get pregnant. You know?"

"We've already been through this, Dad," I said, grimacing. I had hoped we could at least get through breakfast without any unpleasantness. "Your reductive attitudes about gender, reducing it to who does and does not carry babies, are both transphobic and just plain sexist. Maybe if you hadn't reduced Mom down to a fetus incubator, you'd still be together."

His jaw dropped, and his face grew so red under his patchy graying beard that it looked as though I'd just slapped him.

"I'm just telling it like it is, Je..."

I cut him off mid-sentence. "My name is Jason, Dad. Please don't deadname me."

"Oh, right. Yeah, I'm sorry, Jay." He looked befuddled more than apologetic. That, I supposed, would have to do. As would Jay, a legitimate nickname for Jason—but also the abbreviation of my deadname, of which he just would not let go.

"I'm sorry, but... I hate that you said that to me," he growled. "Maria had no right to do what she did to me. No right!"

"Mom didn't do anything to you. She had every right to have an abortion," I hissed back at him. "It's her body. You making it all about you is the problem. And if you had more respect for her personal autonomy, maybe she wouldn't have had to leave you. You're the one who issued an ultimatum, not her."

"You'll never understand," he pouted. "Never in a million years."

"You're right," I said, polishing off the last of my pancakes. "I don't understand. Goodbye, Papa." I threw a twenty down on the floor.

"Leaving so soon?" he asked, eyes blinking rapidly in stunned disbelief. "You just got here, sweetie."

"I have an appointment," I said diplomatically. I was supposed to pick Mom up from UCSF Hospital. Then we were going to hang out in the park for a while. She was going to introduce me to her new boyfriend. Doobie. They just started dating, and she wasn't sure if it was going to go anywhere. Still, she wanted me to meet him. I certainly didn't want to tell Dad that.

Revelation on Hippie Hill

My name is Jason Garcia, but the oldheads down at Golden Gate Park—especially the older queers, but also some friends of my mom that used to follow Phish and the Grateful Dead with her back in the '80s and '90s, before Jerry Garcia died—like to call me Faerie Garcia. I think it's at least partially because of my beard—one of my finest achievements. When I first got on testosterone, I didn't expect it to come in this full—I mean, my dad's never been able to grow this much facial hair. But my mom showed me a lot of pictures of her grandfather and said that's where I got it from. Another reason is because of my long, curly hair. I never cut it and, like my beard, it is bleached and dyed in swirls of blue, green, and purple. I like to call it my merman hair. But the main reason is I remind them of my mother's old friend, Aerie Faerie.

"You never met the original Faerie," Terry Bob, an ex of Mom's, said. His full name was Terrance Robert Johnson, but no one engaged in that kind of formality around here. Some folks called him T. B., and I never thought it was a coincidence that this was also short for tuberculosis. T. B. had dated my mother before my parents were a thing, and although their romance didn't survive his infidelities and heavy marijuana use, they'd remained good friends over the years. He'd helped Mom reconnect with old friends from back in the day after she broke up with Dad. I always suspected it was because he hoped to get back together with her, but Mom had zero interest in another go-around with him. Too flaky and unreliable, and she didn't feel like being twice-burned after the whole cheating thing.

"Aerie was the best," T. B. went on with a reverent nod. "He also loved hair dye. Manic Panic he'd pick up from the old headshop down on the Haight. Mostly hot pink. Used to wear flowers in his hair, like a real throwback to the '60s and the Summer of Love, but with an '80s spin on it, you feel me?"

"Aerie Faerie was my bestie," Mom said, tapping on her knee to the beat of the drum. We sat together on the cool grass on Hippie Hill, feeling nature against the back of our knees. Her crutches were piled on the picnic blanket beside us next to a little picnic basket. I have been my mother's in-home care provider for close to a decade now, since I was in my early twenties. She has cerebral palsy.

Mom is my best friend. We do everything together. That's why I spend so much time with her friends. Honestly, I feel very blessed to be paid to help take care of her. It's my dream job, if you want to keep it real. We were up on an incline, about twenty feet behind the drum circle. The drum circle was centered around two forest-green park benches down below. Although it is called a drum circle, it is not a literal circle. A line of folks sat on the benches, and others sat in a semicircle on the grass across the bicycle path from them. People stood and danced in the grass and behind the benches, leaving a path down the center for the bicyclists to get by.

"He was always playing hacky-sack," Terry Bob said, inhaling deeply from his now-legal medicinal marijuana, cannabis card peeking out of the clear badge holder that he cheekily hung off a shoestring from his neck. Just in case the cops came along. His long, limp hair was strawberry blond somewhere underneath its perpetual layer of grease and dirt. "He always had the best weed, my man. Coolest cat we ever knew. Like, nobody cared that he was gay."

I winced a bit. It was nice that Terry Bob didn't misgender me, but if he didn't care about Aerie being gay, why did he even say that? It was not intentionally microaggressive, but it certainly was awkward.

A half circle of drummers sat on the grass twenty feet below us, with bongo drums between their knees. A brown-skinned man with long dreadlocks, bleached red at the tips by the sunshine, stood slapping a kettle drum that hung over his shoulder by a green, black, and red strap, in time to the rhythm. Mom smiled at him and waved. I wondered if that was Doobie, the new guy she kept talking about?

My quiet reverie was interrupted by a loud smoker's cough, followed by further ramblings by the never-tactful Terry Bob. "Then the AIDS got him!" T. B. bellowed, frowning and shaking his head so hard a dead leaf trapped in his grungy hair shook loose and went drifting down to the grass below. "Too bad he didn't make it 'til the cocktail."

Mom nodded wistfully. "Aerie Faerie passed away in '92, when you were still in diapers. You would have loved him. He was a D&D nerd like you, and a giant science fiction and fantasy fan. He was also one of the people who helped me stand up to my parents." Mom said, fishing a bag of salt and vinegar chips out of her bag. It was right on time. I could hear my stomach rumbling. I started to pull the rest of our snacks out. We had tortilla chips and salsa, and a Tupperware container filled with homemade brownies.

T. B. quickly grabbed one for himself. "They're not the medicinal kind," I told him quickly before he got too excited.

"Bummer," T. B. shot back, inhaling the brownie anyway, in a single bite.

"There's no reason that a person with cerebral palsy can't carry a child to term," Mom said, picking up where she left off. "But my parents were ignorant of the fact. They kept pressuring me to have my tubes tied."

"I never knew that," I said. It was hard to imagine that my doting grandparents hadn't wanted my mother to have any children. But now that she mentioned it, I could remember a few times when I was very young, when Grandma had been strangely overprotective.

"When I met your father, of course," Mom went on, "he really wanted children. And I was glad I'd stuck to my guns. But I made it very clear to him that I only wanted to have one kid. He knew that before we got married."

"He shouldn't have pressured you about the pregnancy," I said, wrapping my arm around her shoulder.

"Joe always was a dick," T. B. said.

I gave him a dirty look. "Cut it out, man. That's my father." My mom gave T. B. that steely kind of side eye that shut people down immediately—the kind that parents seem almost required to learn to keep unruly children in place. T. B. stood up and patted his jeans off.

"Well, I was just about to get going anyway," he said, grabbing another brownie for the road.

"Bye, T. B.," I said. My mother just waved dismissively. T. B. gave her a hug and then scampered off down the hill.

Once he was out of earshot, my mother said, "Honey, I just want you to know that I've been on both sides of this thing... fighting for the right to have a child, and later, fighting for my right to have an abortion. I can't understand what it is like for you as a man. I know there are other considerations for you. But, I just want you to know that, whatever you decide, I will support you 100%. And there are a lot of things about this that I have experienced and can understand."

"All right," I said, smiling. "I love you, Mom."

"Love you too, Jason," she replied with a hug. Just then, the drum circle slowed down and came to a brief stop. The man with the red-tipped dreadlocks nodded to his friends, and turned toward us, hiking up the hill.

"That Doobie?" I asked her with a wink.

"Yes." Mom grinned. "That's the one and only Doobie Douglas."

It's Not Easy Being Green

I'm fortunate enough to live in the San Francisco Bay Area, where I can receive gender-affirming care as a transman. The clinic I go to provides all kinds of services for transgender and gender-nonconforming people. My primary care physician, my therapist, and the staff who gave me referrals for my top surgery all worked here. It was almost impossible to find an ob/gyn who was good with my gender as a transman, and I even had an ob/gyn at the clinic.

But they couldn't do everything here.

I was in the middle of getting referrals for bottom surgery when I found out I was pregnant. I'd known it was a possibility. My partner, Turtle, is capable of producing sperm. But I had thought that it would be very unlikely at most, with me on testosterone. My periods had never gone away entirely, but they'd been fewer and further apart, often amounting to no more than a little bit of spotting.

"You know, you can still get the surgery," my friend Lonnie reassured me on the drive on the way over. Lonnie and I had met in group therapy three years ago and had gotten to know each other very well since. Today, I had given them a ride to the clinic south of Market, as we both lived way out on the edge of town, near City College of San

Francisco. It took like 45 minutes to get here on the bus, and I had the van, which I needed to take Mom around.

"I know," I said easily. "Trust me, I know. But I'm not sure I want to right now. I mean... Turtle wants to keep the baby, and I am considering it."

"It isn't about her, though," Lonnie said, setting their can of lemon-lime soda down in the cup holder. "I mean, I respect that you want to consider her thoughts on the matter, but this is your body."

"I know, I know," I said, shrugging a little. Looking out over the row of neatly painted Victorians that lined the hill separating Cole Valley from the Castro, I could smell eucalyptus on the cool summer breeze. "I mean, it is a lot... I remember after my top surgery, when they first took the tubes out of my chest for drainage, I had all of this dysphoria looking at my stomach, all swollen from the anesthesia. I liked the way my chest looked, but my stomach and hips started to bother me all the more. Little things, like the way my tummy stuck out a bit. And I think, if I keep the baby, that is going to come back, but like ten times over."

"And you don't owe that to anybody," Lonnie reminded me as we arrived at the top of the hill. Looking down, I could see the iconic downtown San Francisco skyline rising along the Embarcadero off in the distance, miles away from here. Halfway between here and there was the clinic, right where the taquerias and richly colorful street murals of the Mission District laced into the nightclubs and clothiers of the South of Market Leather District.

Lonnie took a deep swig from their soda, and we drove for some time in silence. Right as we got within a block of the clinic, they spoke again. "You know, when I first went in to get my hysterectomy, the doctor kept asking me if I was sure. He said that I might change my mind later, and want to have kids. And it made me so mad, you know? I have endometriosis, and it was causing severe monthly pain. He didn't give a shit. All he cared about was me being a future incubator."

"Yuck!" I pulled around the block for the third time. Finally, a parking spot! The cars behind me honked impatiently as I slid into the space. I hopped out of the car, walked around it, and slipped my ATM card into the parking meter.

Lonnie is twenty-seven years old and nonbinary. "He also kept misgendering me, using 'she' pronouns and calling me 'young lady,'" they said.

"Oh, hurl!" I said as we reached the intersection. We weren't in the best part of town, and there were homeless people sleeping on the sidewalk near a chain-link metal fence. The light turned red just as we hit the corner. I sighed, pushing the button on the lamppost for the crosswalk.

"Some people feel having a uterus means you owe the world babies," Lonnie continued.

"Yeah, no shit," I said. "Politicians trying to legislate what we can do with our bodies, forcing us to carry unwanted pregnancies, preventing us from transitioning." The light finally changed, and we crossed the street.

"There weren't any transmen in A Handmaid's Tale, or transmasculine bodies of any kind. But it feels like that. It really does. Like, they feel our transitioning is a threat to their ideas of biological imperative. A kind of biological manifest destiny where their belief system gives them the right to annex our bodies for forcible reproduction.

"It would have been cool if they had transmen in *A Handmaid's Tale*," Lonnie said. "I would like to see that on the TV show, you know?"

A loud, boisterous voice disrupted our conversation. "Lookit, the wearin' o the green!"

Lonnie has a bright green undercut, long on the top, short all the way around the sides. Neither of us is very tall, and we both have at least some green hair. A tall, drunken man with a bright red face, the apparent source of the shouting, was leaning up against the donut shop. He remained silent as we walked past him, but once we were past him, he yelled at our backs, "Look! It's a couple of leprechauns!" as we walked by.

"Do we look fucking Irish to you?" Lonnie shot back over their shoulder.

I laughed. Neither of us are white folks. I added a few choice expletives in Spanish.

Lonnie decided to join in on the fun and curse him out in Vietnamese. The drunken man's jaw dropped.

We shot around the corner and walked into the safety of the clinic.

Turtle the Balladeer

Turtle was waiting for me in the waiting room at the clinic, wearing a frilly purple skirt under a powder-blue T-shirt with a unicorn on the front of it. Knee-high rainbow socks poked out of her well-worn, glittery silver Doc Martens. Her long lilac braids complemented her mahogany complexion, and her deep brown eyes were set off by her daffodil eyeshadow. At her feet sat a guitar case covered in various band stickers, decals with rainbows and narwhals, and political bumper stickers. A large one in the center had "Trans Rights Are Human Rights" emblazoned across a white, pink, and blue trans pride flag.

Lonnie ran up to the counter and checked in for both of us. They grabbed a key off the counter and disappeared into the bathroom.

"Hey, babe," Turtle said, reaching over to give me a hug as I slid into the seat beside her. I gave her a soft but brief kiss on the lips. She leaned over and dropped her head on my shoulder.

"Thanks for coming to the appointment with me," I said.

"I wouldn't miss it," she said gently, taking my hand in hers.

"We're just here to get some information." I wanted to be sure she understood that I still had not made my mind up. "I need to know what exactly to expect before I can make a decision on this. I mean, what would happen to my body, and..."

"Trust me, I understand," she said, hugging me once again. "I just want you to know that your happiness is what matters the most to me here. I don't think you should feel obligated to do anything that makes you uncomfortable. You know?"

"Yeah, I know," I said softly, looking away and grabbing some pamphlets from off the table. "I've been talking to my parents about it this morning, too. My dad, ugh."

"I wrote a song for you," Turtle said with a mischievous sparkle in her eyes. "Want to hear it?" Just then, Lonnie popped out of the bathroom and walked over to where we were seated. They sat across from us and waved.

"The whole waiting room doesn't want to hear it," I said sarcastically.

"I wanna hear it," Lonnie snickered. "And I am pretty sure we're the only ones in here besides the staff."

"Finnnneeee..." I stuck my tongue out at both of them.

Turtle pulled out the guitar, sat it on her knee, and began to gently strum. At first, she hummed along with the tune she was playing. But after a few minutes, she began to sing. "This is the ballad of Faerie Garcia, a handsomer lad you never did see. Eyes deep as canyons, and hair like the ocean. I was lost in those eyes when they first laid on me..."

"Ugh," Lonnie snorted. "I feel like my blood sugar just shot up for some reason."

"When he first laid eyes on me, with his hair like the sea, and his beard wild and free as all mayhem, I said eyes are laid, but would you lay with me, or are ye an exclusively gay man?"

I was snickering loudly by now, and Lonnie was laughing so hard they were starting to slide down the front of their chair onto the floor.

"I like girls and the gays, I go both and all ways, and to you I would never say nay, ma'am," Turtle sang, strumming on her guitar loudly enough to attract the attention of the receptionists, who were exchanging looks, as if trying to determine what to do next.

"He's a handsome young bloke, but our condom, it broke, and that's what brings us both here today, man," Turtle finished, with a great flourish, before quickly returning her guitar to its case.

"Oh laaawwwwd..." the lady behind the reception desk said. The other receptionist tried hard not to laugh but was barely maintaining his composure.

Just then, the door to the back of the clinic cracked open, and Dr. Wong stuck her head out into the waiting room. "Jason Garcia?"

I stood up and walked to the door with Turtle trailing behind, her hand in mine.

Of Bodily Autonomy

"So, I am off my testosterone for now," I told Dr. Wong, my feet kicking nervously over the side of the medical exam table. Turtle sat in a comfortable chair by the door, quietly reading a romance novel. I looked at her meaningfully before I spoke again, but she didn't say a word.

Finally, I said, "I am thinking about keeping the baby. I'm not sure yet, though."

Turtle looked up from behind the book cover. I looked back at her, waiting for her to speak, but she still said nothing.

Dr. Wong caught the exchange and introduced herself to Turtle. "Hi, pleased to meet you... and you are?"

"I'm Turtle," my partner said. "I'm the baby's mother... I mean, I will be if Faerie keeps it, but I told him it's up to him, entirely, of course. His body, his choice. But he does know I want children."

"I wanted Turtle to be here," I said quickly. "I need to know what I am in for before I can decide."

"Of course," Dr. Wong said. "Carrying your pregnancy to term puts your body through certain changes, as does going off testosterone, which you would have to do for the duration of the pregnancy."

I nodded.

"My friend Morton told me that, so I went off right away. He'd gotten off it to get pregnant, and I'd asked him about it."

The Bay Area has a close-knit transgender community, which I am a part of. I've had a strong support system over the past seven years since I first came out. Some of my friends were from groups like Lonnie. Others were from the social scene, like Morton, whom I'd met at a popular queer dance party. Morton's husband was a bi-identified cisgender man, and their pregnancy was very planned. They'd even sought assistance from a fertility clinic, and ended up going the in vitro route to have the baby. We hadn't spoken much since they had successfully conceived a couple of years ago. Our contact consisted mostly of me liking photos of their beaming infant on social media. If I kept this baby, it might make sense to try to rectify that situation by reaching out to them. Bu, when he was pregnant, we talked about it a lot. One of the things he told me was that he had selective reduction, a procedure where some of the zygotes were aborted to avoid having a high-level multiple pregnancy. Even fertility clinics and processes had to involve abortion.

"Is there anything we need to worry about if we decide to keep the baby?" Turtle piped up suddenly. I quickly shot her side eye. She shrugged. Then I sighed. I had asked her here because I wanted her here to ask such questions in case we decided to go that route. But I also wanted to make sure that the questions I had to ask about the effects on my body got answered.

"Not really," Dr. Wong said. "Transmen carrying pregnancies to term have outcomes very similar to ciswomen."

"That's good news," Turtle said. "I mean, if you do decide to keep the baby."

I sighed and gave Turtle a look.

Dr. Wong caught the exchange and said, "Jason. How do you feel about all of this?"

"Still on the fence," I said. "But we still get information."

"I see," Dr. Wong said. "Would you like me to get you some information on prenatal care?"

"Yes, please," I said, foot still ticking nervously against the side of the exam table.

Dr. Wong excused herself for a moment and returned with a stack of pamphlets. She handed them to me. I gave them to Turtle, who stuck them into her guitar case.

"As you know, I want to have bottom surgery," I said. "I'm early in the process, but this was unplanned and unexpected. I need information on how this would affect my transition plans in the short and long terms."

"Even on testosterone, unplanned pregnancies can occur," Dr. Wong said, taking a look at my chart on her computer. "Considering that you have been on testosterone for seven years, you wouldn't experience changes to your voice or more than minor changes to your hair growth. There might be some temporary redistribution of body fat."

"I won't have...Like...you know, my chest would stay the same?"

"You wouldn't experience any regrowth of breast tissue; that's gone forever."

"Oh, yay," I said, relaxing a bit. "And my bottom surgeries?"

"With elective postpartum hysterectomy, you can take your first steps immediately after the birth. And have your phalloplasty a bit further down the line."

"That would be really good," I said, feeling an immediate sense of relief.

"You don't have to make your mind up right now," Dr. Wong said. "But since you might want to carry this pregnancy to term, it's a good idea for you to start taking some blood tests, and for you to get on prenatal vitamins," Dr. Wong said. "Remember, you have options. You can still terminate the pregnancy at any time during the first two trimesters in California. Do you have any other concerns?"

"Yes," I responded, inhaling very deeply, as though I had not been breathing at all for the past ten minutes. "I have a family history of gestational diabetes. My dad told me that this morning."

"Okay, good to know," Dr. Wong said, taking another note. "We should set up a consultation with a nutritionist to assist with preventive care for that. Just remember, preparing for the possibility of carrying the baby to term does not mean that you can't still terminate the pregnancy. You're still pretty early on." She handed me a stack of paperwork ordering the blood tests, and a cup to leave my urine sample in. That concluded our appointment. We went to the desk and got a follow-up appointment for the next week.

Jason's Mom Has Got It Going On

After the doctor's appointment, Lonnie, Turtle, and I drove out to the Haight to hang out with my mom and her friends in Golden Gate Park. This time, we weren't up on Hippie Hill, but over at picnic tables on the grass behind the Golden Gate Carousel. It was a classic old-fashioned wooden carousel, over one hundred years old, having been built in 1914. I could see the lovely painted horses trotting on merry striped steel posts that hoisted them up and down as they circled the old pipe organ. We could hear its sounds playing faintly in the distance.

Bright red plastic tablecloths covered the two picnic tables Terry Bob had commandeered. Matching red plastic utensils glistened in the sun, where they sat piled on a stack of paper plates. In the center of the table was a big white rectangle of cake decorated in blue and yellow florets, with the words "Happy Birthday Maria!" drawn on them in shiny red cursive sugar gel. Novelty candles spelled out, "The Big 50." Mom was sitting next to Doobie, curled under his well-muscled arm. There were a couple dozen other friends of hers milling around the table.

Turtle walked up the table, acoustic guitar dangling from its cloth band, and started playing an old Santana song my mom always loved, "Maria, Maria." Mom smiled, and laughed while Doobie began to thrum his drum in tune. Terry Bob picked an old tambourine off the table and joined in. The vibe was mellow on this warm and sunny day.

When the song came to an end, we all sat at the table and shared tiny bits of our day. And soon Mom and her friends were back to reminiscing about the good old days.

"Your mom always was a firecracker," T. B. said, smiling. "She was out in the streets protesting back in the day. The protestors for the Americans with Disabilities Act were badass. Chaining themselves to government offices. Crawling up the stairs to protest the lack of accessibility for buildings. We were just kids in our teens and early twenties then."

"We took it to the streets," Mom said, laying aside her fork full of cake. "That was the only way to get the government to take notice."

"And even though she was married with a kid," T. B. added with an affirmative nod, "your mom lobbied against that damned third trimester abortion law that passed in 2003."

"Absolutely," Mom said, grinning. "I've also worked from home on the hStopTheBans campaign ever since 2019." Then, she dug into her cake for another bite. It was a simple but tasty vanilla cake with buttercream.

"So, you know, she's okay with whatever you decide," T. B. added.

"I know, I know..." I said, shrugging. I definitely didn't need my mom's ex explaining her politics to me.

"I worked on hStopTheBans, too," Lonnie said excitedly, moving over to take a seat next to my mother. "You may not know this, but I had an abortion in 2018. And when I started reading about all of these people in other states losing access to abortion services, I felt that I needed to take action. Not everyone can live in a state as liberal as California."

"I know," Turtle said, cutting off a slice of cake. "I was really surprised to learn that California has a third trimester abortion ban."

"So was I," I admitted. "What about people who are too poor to access services? Not everyone lives in a town that has Planned Parenthood or a Community Health Clinic to go to for free or low-cost abortions."

"And what about people who don't have regular periods?" Lonnie added. "Not everyone figures out that they're pregnant right away."

I nodded. "We're really lucky to live somewhere where we're safe."

"So, did everything go well at the doctor?" Mom asked, taking my hand.

"Yes, it did," I told my mother. "And I really appreciate everything you've had to say to me. It's been a real education. I had no idea that America had a history of forced sterilization until you told me. I'd always associated eugenics with Nazi Germany."

Turtle raised an eyebrow. "You're Latino. I am surprised you aren't aware of the history of forced sterilization of black and brown people in America. There is a documented history of African American, Latinx, and Native American folks being coerced into sterilization from the 1930s to the 1970s. And, in 2020, reports started arising of ICE forcibly sterilizing detainees."

"That's horrible," Lonnie said, jaw dropping, cake fork momentarily suspended in air. When they regained their composure, they added, "I have known about the forced sterilization of disabled people, which dates back to the early 1900s. I also knew about POCs in the '60s and '70s. I just hadn't heard about ICE."

"Yup," T. B. said, pulling it up on his cell phone and showing it to everyone, as if cell phones had just been invented and using Google made him a technical wizard.

Doobie, who had been silent up until now, said, "You know, me and Maria have been going out to the protests against ICE. Including the one about the forced sterilization of detainees. We might have been involved in some of the same political actions as you all."

I raised my eyebrow. I knew Mom had been going places with Doobie. I had no idea that at least some of these places were protest rallies. "Go Mom!" I said approvingly. Lonnie and Turtle gave her finger snaps to show they approved, and Doobie and T. B. joined in.

"Can we protest with you all sometime?" Lonnie asked my very tickled mother.

Then Mom squeezed my hand again. "So enough about me. Did you get everything you needed at the clinic?"

"I did," I said, almost timidly. "And you're going to be surprised to hear this, but you're gonna be a grandma."

Turtle's eyes widened. "Okay, say that, then! I guess I'm gonna be a mother!"

"Grandma Maria," T. B. said, poking his tongue out at my mom. Doobie quietly gave him the most magnificent and regal side eye I have ever seen.

"I still feel like I am too young to be a grandmother," my mom said with a laugh. "But I will make adjustments."

I grinned and shook my head a little. "Yeah. We're all gonna be making some adjustments. Life sure takes you by surprise sometimes."

The broad subject of reproductive rights includes many things. They should allow for people like me, Lonnie, Morton, and Turtle to make reproductive choices without being constantly misgendered. Reproductive rights include the right to have an abortion. They include the right to opt out of procreation entirely with voluntary sterilization procedures. But they also encompass the right to be free from coerced abortion and forced or coerced sterilization.

EXQUISITE

By Lee Murray

Not what he wants? She stiffens her back. But she can change. She can. Just watch. She clomps home to her apartment, locks the door, and gathers the tools. Begins by breaking her toes, one by one. This little piggy goes to market, this little piggy stays home. It's taking too long; she takes the hammer to them. When they're finally malleable, she plucks out what's left of her nails. Painstaking work, but it'll be worth it.

afternoon sun
glints
through tears

She cracks on, snapping tendons. Binding her feet under. Twisting the fabric tight with a chopstick. Tighter. Yes. She leans back on the sofa and revels in the throbbing. Outside, her sister screams to be let in. He's an idiot, she says. You're more than enough. Except she's not. Not yet. She knows she can be better. If she just bends herself backward. A strip of silk wedged under her chin, knotted behind her knees, and tightened with an umbrella should do it. She hooks the umbrella to the window latch, adding her weight to the gravity. She's nothing, if not resourceful. Her body sags, arm sockets pinging. At last, her spine cracks.

re-threading
her mother's pearls

Outside, it's quiet. The sister has given up banging on the door. With a start, she realizes she didn't think this through. Who is there now to see her transformation from ugly duckling to graceful swan? She can't move to open the door, and with her jaw broken she can't speak. Helpless, she dangles under the window.

on the pond
a crescent moon
reflects

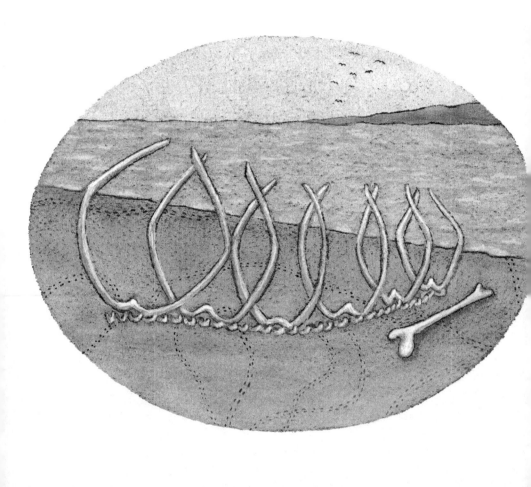

THE LAST, CLEAN, BRIGHT SUMMER

By Livia Llewellyn

This Journal Belongs To:
Hailie

Tacoma, June 15th

I'm writing this in the car. Mom cried again this morning when we left the house. Everything was spotless and put away just like we were going on a vacation for a little while, even though we're not coming back until late fall. She'd been cleaning like crazy since last year, like literally starting on my fourteenth birthday. Dad says she's nesting, because when we come back home, it'll be with a new baby brother, and maybe a sister too. Which totally shocked me, because I didn't even know she was pregnant. There were so many things she wanted to take, but Dad wouldn't rent one of those big RVs, and everything had to fit in our crappy old VW camper instead. So, she just made everything look super neat and nice. I swear, I did more laundry and dishes in the last month than in the last five years! Anyway, so we packed two suitcases and one large backpack each, and got rid of most of the food that might spoil, except for what we're taking (which is currently sitting in paper bags and boxes next to me on the back seat, and all around my feet), and that's it. We pulled out of the driveway early this morning before it was really light, and I turned around and watched my little yellow house disappear. Last night, Dad went out into the backyard with Abby, our dog, to the spot in the back where Alex was. That was the only time I cried.

And now we're on our way down the freeway to Olympia. Dad isn't taking the longer scenic way around the peninsula, but it'll still be a couple of days before we get to the town (which has almost NO internet access, of course), so I brought this journal (even though I'm totally lazy about writing in it) and a couple books. We're going to Oceanside for a humungous family reunion—I was born there, and so was my mom. My parents moved away when I was born, but we used to go back every summer until five years ago, when my younger brother died and my mom said she couldn't do it anymore, at least for a while. I remember we stayed at a really cute cottage inland from Oceanside, a kind of suburban area called the Dunes, where my mother's aunt used to live. She would babysit us while my parents went to the parties—we were always too young to go. I remember it was all shiny wood, and Great Auntie had two huge trunks, one filled with puzzles, and one filled with the most beautiful dolls. And if you stood in the road outside her driveway, you could see past the houses and scrubby trees all the way to the ocean, even though it was almost a mile away. That's how flat it is. That's why the reunion is held there, Dad says, because of the strong tides and the flat beach. Mom doesn't like to talk very much about it. I know she's never liked the reunions, but I'm kind of looking forward to it. I just hope there'll be some interesting boys in town.

Aberdeen, June 16th

This town is super creepy but kind of cool in that weird way. Mom says all the geometry of the architecture here is wrong, and it makes everyone depressed. I have no idea what that means. We stayed the night in a motel just off the highway, and I kept waking up to all the traffic sounds. So, after Mom and Dad were asleep for a while, I got dressed and snuck outside. We were the only ones checked in, and all the other windows were dark. I could see the highway from the balcony, all the lights of the trucks and cars. I just stood there in the dark for a while, listening to the sound of all those cars, watching the red lights stream constantly away.

And then I saw them. I don't know where they came from, but it was like all of a sudden they were just there, standing under the bright yellow parking lot lights. It was two faceless men, although I could barely tell. They were naked except for very tall black top hats, with very shimmery pale skin, all scales, I think, or maybe skin like an alligator. I was so shocked I almost peed my pants! I just stood there frozen, and my skin got all hot and cold like it does when you're so frightened you can't move. They stood there, too, looking up at me. I thought about running, but Dad had said that they weren't dangerous. Just be respectful, and think of them as our summer observers, he had said. Just let them watch us, and we'll all get along just fine. And then they started walking very slowly and gracefully across the parking lot, and I don't know why I did this, but I waved, in a very slow and dignified arc. And they both waved back! I was so happy. And then they disappeared, and I stood there a while longer, watching the car lights twinkling and all the stars rush past me overhead. It was a pretty good night.

This morning before we left Aberdeen, we had breakfast at the restaurant downtown that we used to go to all the time when we came down here, in the old brick building near the factories Dad would visit as part of his job. We all had that awesome French toast, just like we used to, and Mom asked the cook for his secret recipe, and he said no, just like he used to. And then they got in a fight, and Mom was all like, I don't know why you won't give it to me since we're probably the last customers you'll have all summer, and he was all like, well, summer's not over yet and besides, in the fall I'm heading down to South America and taking my recipe with me, and then she was all, it's not South America anymore, you idiot, who do you think is left down there who eats French toast, and then she ran off to the bathroom. The cook grew super angry and quiet, and then my dad took him aside, probably to apologize and tell him Mom's all hormonal and everyone down in Obsidia will totally love his secret French toast.

Mom needs to chill out. She explained what's going to happen at the reunion, that we have to dance around some big-ass dying sea creature in some ancient tribal ceremony to honor our ancestors, and throw some spears into it to "defeat" it, and it's totally not going to be hard at all. It sounds stupid and completely lame.

The Dunes, Oceanside, June 23rd

We're at the cottage now. It's been kind of a strange couple of days. I'm kind of bored and anxious, and I don't know. I guess just it's weird to feel like you're on summer vacation when something so incredible and important is going to happen and you finally get to take part. Mom and Dad are in the town on a dinner date, and this is the first chance I've really had to myself. We got to Oceanside on the 16th. It's straight up the coast from Ocean Shores, but it's a long drive, and the highway gives out to dirt roads and logging roads after a while, and those are a bit hard to find. There were less cars, though. People up here are like us, they're relatives, part of the family, or they're company people like Dad who are cool about everything and stay out of our way. We didn't stop at Ocean Shores, even though I wanted to, but Dad said it was off limits because they'd already done their ceremony and totally fucked it up (his swear word, not mine!) and the town was a total mess. We did stop at this really awesome beach farther up the coast, just outside this huge area of abandoned quarry pits. It's hard to describe how the ocean was there. I mean, there were these waves that were so high and gray and hard, you could feel the beach quake when they crashed down, and they sounded like thunder. They would rise up in the air, and just hang there like they were alive, like they were waiting. For what, I don't know. All the sand was pure black, just like in parts of Hawaii, and we found a skeleton of some huge whale thing that was about as long as our old neighborhood road. Dad kept calling it a kraken, which was hilarious. Mom got pretty excited when she saw it and took all kinds of pictures and had us all pose next to the skull. I sat in the eye socket. Yeah, it was kind of neat! I was just happy to see Mom so happy. It was sunny and warm out, and there were gulls everywhere and the funniest-looking crabs.

Anyway, so we got to Oceanside in the late afternoon, when the sun was setting over the Pacific, and the sky was pink and orange and red, and the air smelled all sandy and salty like brine. Dad drove down the main street and parked next to the chowder house where we'd have dinner, and we got out and stood in the middle of the road. Just like near the cottage, you'd usually be able to see all the way to the ocean, it would look like the road just kept going on through the beach and then under the waves. Except, not anymore, because of the wall. Dad's a really important architect, and he helped design this for Oceanside and for other towns all up and down the coast that are having family reunions, whenever it's their time. Except Ocean Shores, of course, and a couple other places that didn't build a wall and got destroyed. Mom took more pictures, and then we went inside.

We got to the cottage after dark. It was exactly like I remembered it—all the nautical stuff everywhere and the flowered couch that turns into a bed. Mom got teary-eyed when she saw the trunks of toys, but she covered it up and fussed around in the kitchen with the food, while Dad and

I pretended not to notice. I'll admit, I got a bit sad when I saw the puzzles, too. I remember Alex and me putting them together on the rickety cardboard table Great Auntie set up for us. That was the last summer before he started getting sick. It was the inoculations. All the men in our family start taking it when they're about nine to fight some infection they're not immune to when they grow up, but sometimes they'd have allergic reactions to it, and it would do terrible things to their bodies, like it did to Alex. Dad felt so guilty, but how could he have known?

Anyway, it's been quiet. There aren't any interesting boys here at all. They're all at the wall, I guess, along with the men. I've been spending the days with my mom, and some of the other relatives and their daughters, who I guess are my cousins, reading and getting a tan in their yards. No one cool is around here. None of my cousins are interesting. One girl didn't even know who Beyoncé was! I brought my good bikini for nothing.

The Wall, Oceanside, July 5th

Yesterday was the Fourth, of course, and all over the Dunes, there were lots of backyard parties and barbeques. I finally met a few cute boys, but they were all my cousins, of course, and they wouldn't even talk to me and were pretty rude. Of course, we all ate dinner in the afternoon because when it got dark, everyone in the town and from the Dunes met at the wall. It was insane. We all walked down the long main road, no one was in their car, and none of us were allowed to bring our cameras or phones. Most of the lights were off, except for some crazy lamps in a few store and restaurant fronts, these large circles of glass that glowed a deep green. They were so pretty and strange. I kept looking down at my skin—it looked like it was being lit from inside. All the women and the girls looked like that. All the boys and men were dressed in black suits, even though it was really hot. I mean, this is the middle of summer, after all. A lot of them didn't look very happy about it. But it's tradition, Dad says. It's part of the reunion. And another tradition is that this was the one night all the men escorted the women to the top of the wall, the only time we were allowed to be up there. Well, I'm sure the tradition started out as another night, but having it on the Fourth of July probably gave them an excuse for all the fireworks and beer.

When we got to the wall, the men escorted us single file inside, up these long narrow corridors of stairs that go to the top. It was kind of like a school fire drill in reverse. There were no lights in the stairs, and I pretty much had to climb them with my hands and feet like a dog. I have no idea who was behind me, but I'm glad they couldn't see my butt in their face. When we got to the top, there were about ten observers waiting for us like the ones I saw in the parking lot, naked and faceless with high top hats. I couldn't tell if some of them were the same ones from the parking lot. They didn't look so friendly close up. Everyone grew really quiet and still. We all stood in line around the curved edge, all the women in front so they could see over the metal railing, and the men behind them. I wanted to see the town because we were so high up, but the guy behind me grabbed me and forced me to turn back around. What an asshole.

Anyway. We all stood there for a few minutes in the dark. If we were supposed to be looking at something, no one said. No one spoke. The beach was black, with that same sand Dad and Mom and I had found by the quarry site, but here it was smooth and completely bare. I didn't realize how high the wall was, but it's enormous, so wide that all of us—maybe close to a thousand people—can stand on it, and the beach that it circles around is huge. The waves were farther back than I remember, or at least farther back than they were by the Dunes, and they were massive. I was shocked. If they'd been any closer, they would have come right over the wall. They would rush in toward the wall like a herd of gigantic animals, like serpents made out of water and foam, and I felt everyone sort of gasp and shrink back all at once, me included, and then they'd come crashing down, dragging the sand away and leaving the beach smooth and clean.

So, we watched for a few more minutes, and then the fireworks started over the town, and everyone turned to the other side of the wall and oohed and awed. It was a pretty good show. I kept turning back to the beach, though. Having my back to those waves made me a bit nervous. I bent over the railing slightly to get a better view of the beach and the bottom of the wall. I don't know how we're expected to get down there for the ceremony—I couldn't see any stairway openings, and the wall goes right into the ocean, for a really long way. Maybe we take boats around the edges? I don't know. And then the fireworks were over, and everyone went back down the steps. There were some parties in town at the bars and restaurants, but Mom and Dad went home with me instead. The neighbors down the road were having a big pool party, which seems really redundant (having a pool, that is) when you live next to the ocean but whatever, so I knew they'd go there. Mom asked me if I had any questions about the beach, and I said no, but I was lying. I don't know, I didn't want to talk about it. Mom put her arm around me and said everything would be fine. Funny, when just three weeks ago, she was the one having complete kittens about the reunion.

When we got to the edge of the Dunes, Dad tapped my shoulder and told me to look around. All along the wall, those green globe lamps had been placed. You could see this huge curve of weird green lights hovering in the air between the town and the beach, all of them flashing like little lighthouse beacons or the lights along a runway. He asked me if I thought that was cool, and I said yeah, awesome, or something like that. And that's when I really started to bug out about this whole reunion thing, and felt my skin grow all hot and cold and shivery again, although I acted like I was totally chilled out and fine.

Here's the thing. When I was staring out at the ocean, when everyone else was looking at the fireworks, I saw something. I swear I saw something. Way far off in the ocean, past all the waves, it was in the moonlight, just for a second, and then it was gone. It wasn't an orca or a blue whale. I've seen those tons of times before. I swear to god I saw a gigantic hand.

The Dunes, July 11th

Nothing has been happening. I guess it'd be a great vacation, if it were a vacation, if I didn't have this constant ball of anxiety inside that makes me double over in pain every once in a while. It's really hot now, almost 85 every day. I go to the neighbor's house most days, and lie on a blanket by the pool listening to my iPod or reading. I've got a great tan. Mom goes with me and gossips with the other women, or sometimes we'll go into Oceanside and just walk around, shopping for trinkets or clothes at the little stores, buying magazines, eating lunch at the one café. When we're outside, walking down the narrow sidewalks, I'll try so hard not to, but I always look up at the wall. I can't help it. The lights are still flashing, day and night, and sometimes there's a huge booming sound, and the ground shakes a little, like the waves are reaching the wall and trying to knock it down. Most of the men from the town and the Dunes are up there, and a lot of observers, too. Dad spends every day there. He doesn't talk about it, and I am so relieved that he doesn't. We'll have dinner—Mom's teaching me how to cook. I made spaghetti last night!—and then we'll watch TV if the reception is good, or play board games, or go over to a relative's house and hang out. No one talks about the wall. Sometimes I'll look up and catch a bunch of Mom and Dad's friends or relatives looking at me, and they'll stop talking and look away. They do this with all the girls. Super creepy.

Last night I snuck outside and tried to take a picture

of the lights, but something's wrong with my phone, it doesn't work at all. I think it's broken. This summer blows.

The Dunes, July 23rd

I'm so tired, but I can't get to sleep. Dad just left. It's about midnight, and maybe about an hour ago, some men knocked on the door, and Dad spoke with them for a few minutes, and then he changed into his black suit and left. He told us it's almost time, and to get a good night's sleep, and early tomorrow morning the men would come for us, and the ceremony would begin. I kind of freaked out a little, but Mom calmed me down, then she poured us both a small glass of wine—my first ever!—and she got all teary-eyed again and gave a little speech about how everything was going to change and tomorrow I was going to become a woman (GOD! so embarrassing) and how she was so proud of me and that she knew that no matter what happened, someday I'd be a wonderful mom. The wine tasted terrible. I thought wine was supposed to taste like fruit, but she made me drink the whole glass. I feel a little gross now, kind of floppy and fuzzy. I keep thinking about Alex. I think about his skeleton, under our backyard, all twisted and spiraled and decayed. And Abby, my big-eyed pug, her little skull filled with worms and dirt.

Why do all the men wear top hats?
Why do I hear horns?

The Dunes, August 29th

Wow. I lost a month.

The cast has been off my arm for a couple of days now, and even though the fingers are a bit stiff, I can finally write again without bursting into tears. When I say that, I mean I can write without my fingers hurting, and I can write about what happened without tears rolling down my face, without dropping my pen to the floor, staring off into space, at the wall, through the window, staring anywhere except my journal, where I have to remember what happened and put it into words. Which I guess we're not supposed to do—that is, the women aren't supposed to do this, make records of anything. But I think I should, for reasons I won't go into just right now. I just think it's important to remember, to have a record of my own. Mom and Dad have gone into town for the afternoon to check on my new sisters, so I'm all alone.

So, this is what happened.

THE BEACH, July 24th

I don't remember falling asleep. It was the wine, Mom explained later. The men put a little something in it to help us sleep. It just makes it easier for everyone.

I woke up in a cage, naked. My head was against Mom's thigh, and she was stroking my hair like she used to when I was a little girl. The cage was iron or steel, and it was covered with thick canvas and fastened underneath the bottom, so you couldn't lift it or see outside no matter which way you looked. I could smell the salt of the ocean, and hear the rumble of waves. I knew we were outside, right on the beach, but it sounded far away, like at low tide in the morning. I felt really disoriented. I sat up and tried to ask Mom what was happening, but she shushed me. She was naked too. I was so embarrassed, I wanted to die. Then, she whispered to keep quiet, and just do everything she and the other women did. She said if we got separated and I got confused or afraid, my instincts would tell me what to do.

The canvas rose up—and the smell hit us, not just of the ocean but the low tide stench of something leviathan and dying. I heard a couple girls vomit. The wall was on one side of our cages, and the beach on the other. It was early morning, so early that the sand and water and sky looked all the same color, sort of a flat dark blue. Something was on the beach, white and malformed. I guess I thought it was a whale at first—what else could be that big? And then I realized it was an ocean liner—no whale could be that huge. Mom pushed at the cage, and one side swung open. All around us, against the curve of the wall, cages were opening, and women and their daughters were stepping out onto the sands—maybe five hundred of us in all. We were all barefoot, and all naked and shivering in the cool air. I squinted and turned my head, and that's when I realized. It was so large, I hadn't recognized it at first. But then, yes. I'd seen it before.

It was a woman. A woman so massive I couldn't see the ends of her legs. They were still in the water, the waves lapping at her knees. Her arm was stretched out, her fingertips almost touching the row of cages. That was the hand I knew I'd seen at the ocean's edge that night, pale and grasping in the distant moonlight. We started to walk down the beach toward her face, some of us running. Long blue-green hair like seaweed spread across the black beach. She lay on her back, face to the side, saucer-wide eyes open. She didn't look like some hideous fish creature. She looked like any of us. She looked like me. I could feel the heat of her breath. She was beached but alive, barely. And her stomach! It rose up like Mount Rainier, white and round and full.

She's pregnant, I whispered to Mom, and she nodded. *Are we supposed to dance around her?* I asked.

Not quite. We have to help her give birth, she replied. *But before that, we need to be brave. There's something very difficult we need to do.*

An object slid off the woman's belly and dropped onto the sands. I almost didn't see it at first; it was the same color as her mottled flesh. It rose up from the sand, and everyone jumped back a bit. Another object slid down her belly, and one more slithered out from under her breast. All across her body, I could see movement, hundreds of ripples breaking free. Mom grabbed my arm, hard, so I couldn't run. All around me, the women were whispering to the girls, holding their arms.

Don't fight them, Mom whispered. *And don't run. Just let them do what they need to do.*

What are they? I asked.

I don't know. Maybe the men know. They ride her body up to the surface of the ocean, and now they're waiting for her babies to be born.

Babies? I asked.

She has eggs, hundreds of female eggs, and when they hatch, they'll be waiting for the girls.

To eat them, I said?

No, Mom said. *To spawn.*

From beside me, a high-pitched scream. I saw a girl break free and start to run, and then we all screamed, the thin sounds bouncing back and forth across the wall. I punched my mother in the stomach and pushed her away. We all ran. We ran as fast as we could across the soft slow sands back to the cages, and it didn't make any difference. None of us were fast enough, and none of us were strong. Something grabbed my hair and flipped me up high in the air like one of my auntie's dolls. I came down flat on my back, and it was on me in a flash—soft squishy skin and sucking mouth and the smell. And it was hammering into me, with its huge hard lumpy thing that hurt so much I cried and threw up, and it licked my face and stuck its flappy tongue in my mouth and I threw up some more and choked, and it just wouldn't stop pounding against me, and I felt my right wrist snap under its grip, and the sudden pain made everything bright and calm and clear. I lay still, and the creature fucked me over and over, and I looked up at the iron sky and waited for the sun to break over the wall.

And after a while, it stopped and rolled off me, shuddering and flopping like a giant fish. I lay on the sands with my legs open, mouth open, watching it die. All around me, girls and women were fighting and screaming, the grunts and groans filling the air, the smell of rancid water and vomit and semen and chum. Everyone sobbed. I sat up slowly. Every muscle in my body hurt, every bone felt broken or bruised. Already, half of the creatures were dying or dead. Some were fighting viciously over girls, tearing off each other's limbs with thick claws and lantern-jawed teeth. I didn't know where my mother was, but I didn't want to look. Next to me, a girl lay half buried in the sand. I recognized her from the Dunes. Her head was caved in, the dead creature's thing still resting in the broken nest of teeth spilling out of her mouth.

I would have thrown up again, but I was completely empty inside.

Behind me, the cages started to clatter. I turned around, keeping my head low. Large knives were falling onto the tops of the cases, some of them bouncing onto the sands. Long, sharp butcher knives and machetes. Nets followed, huge fishing nets slithering down like punctured balloons. I stared up at the wall. In the growing light, I could see some of the men hurling the knives down the long curve of stone. The rest of them stood at the railing, writing notes in books, talking to the observers, staring down at us through telescopes and binoculars. And then I saw. Most of the men had their penises out. They were masturbating. They were watching us, watching their wives and their daughters scream and break apart and die on the beach just like that giantess, and they were masturbating through the metal rails as if it were the most exciting thing in the world.

I felt a hand on my foot, and I whipped my leg back, swallowing my scream. My mother, crawling past me. *Grab a knife and a net,* she said. *We have to harvest the eggs.* I watched her move past me, blood on her broken nose, blood trickling between her legs. *My arm is broken,* I said. *Then, use your other arm.* She threw a machete at me, and it landed against my legs, slicing open my skin. I glared at her, but she just walked past. I followed her, limping, tears running down my face. *That's for the punch in the stomach*, she finally said.

When does the dancing start, I said.

Don't start that shit with me, she replied. She didn't look back, only kept walking toward the giantess. The other older women were limping and crawling to the cages, grabbing knives, helping the younger girls get up, heading down to the large stomach. Some of them were walking around, sticking their knives into the creatures that weren't quite dead. Some of them stuck them into the girls.

My mother walked down to the woman's neck. Her breath was so shallow now, she was almost gone. She wasn't moving at all. I stopped in front of her eyes. I'd never seen such large eyes in my life, and the colors—I can't describe them. Like no colors on Earth, and the colors moved and shifted like strands of jewels dancing in starry waters. I think she saw me. I'll never know. She gave a shudder, and one long sigh, and then I could tell she wasn't staring at me or anything else on the beach anymore.

Come on. My mother, standing in a river of blood, her machete and half her body red and wet. *You killed her*, I said.

She was dying anyway. She comes here to give birth on the beach and die. that's what her kind does.

And she gives birth to us? That's how we were born?

Mom nodded. *That's right. We don't give birth to girls. We're not allowed. And this thing,* she pointed to the body, *only gives birth to females. So, I got you here, and my mother got me here, when we came out of the ocean in someone like this, many years ago.*

But Dad said we'd be coming back with a boy, remember? That you were going to have a boy.

Mom pointed to one of the creatures. *That's what he does. That's what he's good for, every time. Next year, we're both giving birth, and we can keep them if they're boys.*

In the distance, the women let out a shout. They had split open the stomach with their machetes, and masses of blood and placenta were spilling across the beach. Inside the thick gore, round objects, no larger than beach balls, rolled and spun.

But Mommy. I was starting to cry. I didn't understand what she was saying, what she meant. I placed my broken hand against my stomach. *I'm pregnant? What happens if I'm pregnant with a girl? What happens to the girl babies if we're only allowed to have boys?* And Mom let out this long sigh like I was just SO stupid, and gave me a funny, tight grin, and said, *What makes you think your brother and your dog are the only bodies buried in the backyard?* And she walked away from me toward the eggs, dragging her empty net.

I walked back up to the woman's outstretched hand, and stood there for the longest time, my five small fingertips against the massive whorls of her rough skin, thinking about all the smooth flat rocks I sat on and skipped across in our backyard, and all the times when I was really little and Mom wore those pretty loose-fitting dresses and how instead of hugging her, she would only let me hold her hand. And then the sun broke through the gray clouds, and it was really low in the sky, and everything just lit up so lovely and bright, all the black sand and the steaming red mounds of organs and the white hills of flesh everywhere and the woman's beautiful dimming eyes. Wide rivers of shit and afterbirth and viscera blossoming into dark clouds as they slid under the waters. And those eggs being packed into the nets and dragged up to the empty cages, those gross pink sacs that we, that I, were stealing out of the dead giantess, that a bunch of strangers would be mothers to for the rest of their lives. Just like all the women on the beach. Just like me. And all the seawater and semen running down my purpling legs, and now the walls opened up and men in hazmat suits came out with giant axes and bone saws and ran toward the body, and wet shards of the dead giantess spurted into the bright morning sky, and the seagulls went joyfully insane.

And I looked up at the sunlit wall, all those black-suited men and boys staring and talking about the other women and me, still making their little observations and notes, still with their cocks in their hands, laughing and staring down. And this was the beach I was born on, the beautiful beach of my childhood, and everywhere I looked, there was nothing but grime and foam and ugliness and death.

And that was the end of summer.

The Dunes, August 29th

Anyway. Yeah, so. Family reunion.

I don't know what happened to all the parts of the giantess's body. More men came, and carted everything away, and then they worked nonstop on dismantling the wall. It'll be shipped off to some other town that needs it next. We'll be driving back to Tacoma in a couple of days. And then school starts, which is just so weird to think about that I can't even. Funny, though, how all the boys I could never find all summer long or who were never interested have suddenly shown up, hanging around the cottages of me and the other girls, totally paying attention, totally competing for us, making sure we don't forget them when we're gone. Even the man who pretends to be my father looks at me strange when the woman who calls herself my mother isn't around, although I stare him down so hard he knows he'd never fucking dare. I don't know, now that everyone knows I'm pregnant, maybe they think I'll be a good wife, a good mom to what they hope will be their son. Yeah, everyone wants a good catch. Or maybe they're just pretending. Maybe they're keeping track of me like they were on the wall. Maybe they're afraid of what I'll do to them if their backs are turned, what I'll do to them like the wave of a hard ocean storm.

Someday.

DAMSEL IN DISTRESS, REDUX

By Marsheila Rockwell

Her tower window
A knight below
Spinning tales of courtly love
Promising her freedom
She does not let down her hair

Spurned and sour, he rides away
She watches him go without regret
The wise princess knows
Rescues unasked for
Only forge new chains

BETWEEN ORIGIN AND DESTINATION

By Marguerite Reed

Sit down. I'm going to talk about abortion today.

Oh good lord, no, I'm not going to beat you over the head with every slogan you've heard, or some you haven't. Nor am I going to show you those photographs, garish and confrontational to the point of terrorism.

Those photos and placards are antiques anyway. Who needs them now that the law has been built up, brick by brick, to protect all those pregnancies? There's even a special force back home—some chimera of law enforcement and social work—that monitors pregnancies. Every single medical professional, no matter whether an acupuncturist or a xenobiologist, is required to keep records of all reproductive activity of their patients. But past that, to catch—I mean monitor—people who don't go to doctors is very simple. Track them with credit usage, net searches, viza-vee work—it's child play.

Forgive the pun.

In the earlier days, some hopeful politicians declared there should be a similar monitor on sperm activity, but that was for theatrics. Can you imagine a squad of cops showing up to some student's room to put zip ties on him after he ejaculates into his girlfriend's underpants? I can imagine it—but only as satire.

By the time I started medical school, new wonders, new

wars assailed us. Death came knocking, and instead of making a place for it at the table, we barred the door. We insulated everything ourselves, and when we looked again, we saw too late that what we thought were swaddling cloths were actually the linen bandages for mummies.

"But Dr. Castaneda," you're going to say, "you're an obstetrician. You *deliver* babies."

Absolutely, I do—did. And on that ship, I was one of the most important people around, even considering the tech captain and the genetiphysicist. Every pregnancy was fraught with danger. Danger not only to the fetus, but to the childbearer, to the entire shipboard's biosphere.

Space doesn't forgive. It's not like water, which we can comprehend, even though our forbearers practiced weightlessness in water. Water is all about weight, and pressure. There's still an abundance of gravity in water, as well as the nutrients, the chemicals that we, as a species, evolved with. Space has none of that. Generation ships have been called the womb of the new human experiment—but don't forget, the uterus is to protect the gestator from the thing it is gestating.

Although space does a pretty fair job of protecting itself. Remember the great radiation horror of '72? Those poor kids recalled from Mars—well, I call them kids, but they weren't kids by the time we got them back. No, none of them recovered. So many pixels published on all the possible ways that might have turned out, and I still don't know whether it would have been a better choice for them to stay on Mars and die. But the de facto leader of that doomed little group said, "No way, sibs, let's get home." He took them back to Earth to sink into the heavier gravity, into the sea of nitrogen and oxygen and bacteria loads that we as a species evolved with. Perhaps on an impulse akin to the one I experienced as a child upon finding a dying insect on the sidewalk, placing it on the grass, or in the heart of a flower, where it came from—to die in what I hoped was kindness.

I was a morbid child, and full of pity.

That ship held five thousand embryos in (what we hoped was) perfect stasis. What you heard is true: Some of those embryos were clones of donors. Unable to take the journey due to age, health, or other reasons, they had spent dizzying sums of money to generate a clone of themselves and then another dizzying sum in "scientific donations." What? Of course they signed informed consent. They were told ad nauseum that a clone wouldn't be exact reproductions of themselves, and the technology for uploaded memories is still in its infancy. Heh. But hope is a light that blinds as well as illuminates. Someday, perhaps, your children will learn how those clones worked out.

So, the embryos. We knew some of them would end up non-viable; that's why there were so many of them. There was an even greater collection of frozen eggs and sperm. A crew that needed neither light nor oxygen, but one that consumed resources all the same. And then the other crew—those lucky bitches who were selected for torpor. Medically induced hypothermia. While they used more resources than the eggs and embryos, they consumed no solid food, and their oxygen use was less than we crew of the first leg, we doulas, if you like, of this great pregnancy. The more a generation ship diverted its resources, the smaller the chance it had of reaching its destination. Of the human cargo surviving.

This will sound facetious, possibly: I think the greatest resource devoured by all those potentialities, those frozen hopes, was our attention. Of course, the tech captains monitored the ship itself, hyper-focused on the second-to-second relay of data from all sensors. Without them, there would be no point in survival. But without our cargo, there would be no point in their stewardship of the Kybele.

We were a hive of drones and workers constantly tending our larvae. All of us sterile. Or so we thought.

While my position was Chief of Telobstetrics, I also

served adjacent to the gynecology and andrology divisions. We rotated often; remember, redundancy was key. Specialization was a luxury. So, it was not uncommon for me to see the women of the crew for routine checks. On the Kybele, routine was a word with positive connotations. Anything out of the ordinary equaled diversion of resources.

And five minutes after Specialist Keely Onopka walked into the exam room, I saw our millenium-long dream shrink down to nothing.

Like most of us on the ship, Onopka was of an economic build. Just under average height, enough body fat, dark hair, olive skin. Good protection against the sun's ultraviolet light on Earth. But in space, no one can tan. Every six months, she, and all the other crew had a full physical exam, and in addition to labs, a full body scan was done. The human body is a buffet for carcinogenic radiation, you know. Juicy little cells, wide open to mutation, growth, and absolute disdain for apoptosis. Onopka's thirty-one-year-old body up to this point had chugged along in exemplary fashion. Yet, as I wanded the transducer over her abdomen, I saw the great machine of reproduction obeying biology's diktat.

"Specialist Onopka," I said, peering at the monitor. "How've you been feeling? Anything out of the range of normal?" Standard question.

"Everything five." She shrugged. The black-and-white images heaved and reformed. "I'd like to know if there can be some kind of rule on how much cologne can be worn by crew, though. People seem to be overdoing it lately. And breath! Do we need to have another dental hygiene week? You know, I thought smells in space would be a lot more subdued."

There it was, looking like a kidney bean. The weight of that little bean tumbled slivers of the future over like the glass fragments in a kaleidoscope. Patterns changed. After a moment, I could speak. "You maintaining caloric parameters?"

"I've cut back a little bit—I've been feeling tired lately, so I was slacking on my exercise, and I've put on maybe a kilogram. Gotta fix that." She frowned. "See something, Doc?"

"I'm afraid I do." There was no way to soften this. "I see an embryo."

Onopka's frown smoothed out, but her gaze burned. "I don't understand. You—you didn't say *an embryo*, did you?"

"About seven, eight weeks along, by the looks of it."

"Let me see."

I turned the monitor and pointed out the uterus, which resembled a fat outline of a thumb and forefinger, indicating *just a little bit*. Just a little bit pregnant. Just a little bit of a problem.

Onopka looked at the image for a long moment. "All right. I want an abortion."

"Well," I said, and then stopped. Took a breath. "I can't."

"You absolutely can. You have to; you *know* you have to." Onopka pulled down her tunic, covering her torso, and stepped off the imaging pad. She stabbed her arms into the sleeves of her uniform coat, jerked it snug around her shoulders, and snapped the buttons. "This can't be happening. Damn it, I had a ligation. And he had a vasectomy."

"Sometimes the tissue grows back together." From the expression on her face, I gathered my comment was unhelpful.

"This isn't some fucked-up fake, is it? A replay of an actual pregnancy?"

"To what end?"

"I don't know! I don't *know*..." She raked her fingers through her hair, and paused, holding her skull as if to prevent it from splitting apart. "It would make more sense to hide a pregnancy from me—for *research*."

"It would be unethical for me not to tell you you're pregnant."

"It's unethical for you to tell me I'm pregnant and then

prevent me from doing a damned thing about it!" She gestured at the scanner, the bank of computer files stored on the wall. "The whole purpose of this is to detect any problem with the crew's bodies, right? Effects of long-term space travel? And if I came in here with cancer—which is abnormal cell growth, just like what we're seeing on this screen—you would remove it and dispose of it."

"I would."

Would I, though? If a blood test had come back positive for markers, if I'd found a mass or lesion—I weighed it in my mind. Would I have told her? What difference would it have made? What was the disadvantage of her treatment set against the disadvantage of her death? Would I let her die in agony and bewildered shame, hiding the truth from her until it was too late? Hypothetically, it would be a huge supply of data for the future. But by keeping her in ignorance, I removed her free will. Was informing her of something so momentous and still withholding her options any different?

"Then why can't you? Why can't you remove it and store it with the others?"

"Which embryo should I remove to make way for yours?"

"There's no spares?"

"None."

"Couldn't you create, I don't know, twins?"

At my expression, she caught herself and shook her head. I pressed forward. "The embryos in storage are what we have, and all we have."

"All we have," Onopka repeated, and laughed sourly. "I'm in one of those quad berths, you know them? With three other women. We share everything; we take turns. Like everyone else on this ship. I guess I should tell them I'm sharing a baby with them, too."

I could have told her there was precedent for that—not on a generation ship, of course, but in the hope-posts on Mars. Only the communists had survived there and in the habitats on Europa.

"We have to get the people to pilot Kybele from somewhere, you know."

"Don't I know that? I'm supposed to teach them! It says so in my ForwardPlan file!" Suddenly, she struck herself, her belly. I winced and winced again at her next words. "I can't be who I'm supposed to be with this parasite inside me!"

She turned to me, eyes gone dark, her beautiful skin sallow with shock and stress. "If you can't do it, Doctor, I'll do it myself."

Yes, I know how to do an abortion. Difficult? No, but you have to pay attention. I was one of the last physicians in the country who had been trained and was willing to teach. In order to teach, however, an instructor has to have students. And on Earth, medical students were too afraid to train with me. Plenty of women would have been happy to take their place in secret, but I couldn't risk that. If the legislators who drew up the regulations for Kybele had consulted me, I would have ensured the right to abortion. Even of our preserved embryos—there was always a chance that something might go wrong.

Why couldn't I perform an abortion? The law. The code of Kybele, which prohibited the taking of not just any life, but specifically the lives of any of those frozen zygotes. The charter had made it very clear that they were our bond with the future, our pledge to the survival of the human race.

On Earth, as a gynecologist, I had performed abortions. I was one of the last practitioners in the country. Laws restricting provision of women's medical care—obstructing every aspect from cancer detection to breast feeding to menstruation—had proliferated throughout the last century. Completely antithetical to the advances in the century previous to that, advances which sought to free women from the feedlots of civilization. To unfetter their legal status, their economic ability, their political viability.

In the eyes of some, that had worked too well, and so women's bodies became a battleground. Never mind the right to vote, did women have the rights to their own bodies?

Easily, such questions led to murder.

In Kybele—and the world beyond—we wanted to build a better society, did we not?

So many pregnancies result in miscarriages. Statistics quoted one number, but knowing human nature, I was sure the number was greater. Unreported. These days, reporting a miscarriage on Earth was not only a medical requirement but a legal one as well. Onopka carrying her baby to term would mean a victory of sorts—a sign. At least that's how the ship's propaganda would spin it.

It wasn't as if we didn't have children on board, but they'd been born before Kybele launched. Their children would be the ones to truly be orphaned of Earth. Before Kybele, multiple conferences weighed the morality of forcing a population to be born into a cruelly limiting experiment. "After all," one panelist said, "the children born on board the Mayflower could always go back."

"And the children born on the Middle Passage could not," snapped another. "Not everyone's voyage to a new world is the same."

Every so often, I'd go to one of the garden parks close to my quarters and watch the children playing. They played like any other children I'd seen, chasing each other, working out some complicated game with a ball, jumping, hand-clapping, and producing an incredible amount of noise. Healthy bones. Healthy lungs. Healthy eyes. A seven-year-old took anywhere from eighteen to thirty breaths a minute, and a newborn took thirty to sixty. A healthy adult took between twelve and eighteen breaths a minute—and required somewhere around two thousand three hundred liters of oxygen a day, with a production of around a kilogram of carbon dioxide. The Sabatier–Bosch reactors scrubbed ceaselessly, a closed system separating and recombining molecules into other molecules. Water. Hydrogen. Methane. Oxygen.

Systems within systems, precariously and perfectly balanced. And now, Onopka's system had been unbalanced. Internal fertilization and implantation could be looked at as a form of parasitism, with the parasite encysted in the host's body and feeding from the host's resources.

Technology has given us the ability to become a species that has switched reproductive strategies: from K-selection, which refers to having only a few children with energy spent on protecting and raising the young, to r-selection, where the energy is spent on producing as many young as possible instead of spent in care for the young post birth. It's possible to inseminate all of a human female's eggs and develop them up to parturition.

My vocabulary? What's wrong with my vocabulary? Did I use profanity? I see. Let me rephrase: Being pregnant is a lot like having a tapeworm. It feeds off you. But with a uterus that's outside the body, the wear and tear are minimized to almost nothing, and theoretically a woman can have as many babies as she has eggs.

I suppose that's the reproductive strategy we'll need when we finally get to this planet. I should say you, not we. I'll be dead by then, and all the adults you know. There's a good chance you'll still be alive. Maybe. Just keep that radiation amount monitored.

Do you understand my position at all? I pored over the charter for the Kybele on top of all my other scheduled tasks; I turned down Connection Time and a Fuck Date—you don't call them that anymore? You call them Fizzens? Oh—physical encounters. PhysEns. Well, that has all kinds of amusing potential for wordplay.

To return to the matter, I immersed myself in Kybele law. All kinds of provisions have been made, you know, for fetuses. You and your packaged generation are the most alarming and studied group ever—the link between worlds, you know? All assigned to trad couples, same-sex couples, mixed- or same-gender polycules. The kids at the other end of the tunnel—less than a century now—they'll be wild. If you live to see them, you'll want to protect them with rules and walls, and there'll be some who obey. There'll be those who don't obey, and Our Lady help you then.

Yes, right, the law. There were no laws about pregnancy. Which meant no laws about abortion, except the laws condemning anyone who through willful interference caused the demise of one of these fetuses. Who would do such a thing? No idea. Still, the law was there, and I had lived through so much trouble back on Earth with regard to abortion. I was reluctant to court any of that in this closed community.

The next day, Onopka burst in on me, in the middle of seeing a patient about a yeast infection. Fortunately, I'd heard her and the medical assistant shouting at each other before she opened the door, so I wasn't caught in mid-swab. My patient, however, nearly boxed my ears with her knees.

"Keely!" she yelped. "What the hell?"

"Just decomp, Nola," Onopka said. "Doc, I need to talk to you."

"You can wait like everyone else." I got the swab while PO Bernard was distracted. Inflamed, with a light discharge; the poor kid was suffering from either candida or bad sex. I could help the one, but not the other.

"Remember what I said, that I'd do it myself?"

I put the swab in the labeled specimen packet, sealed it, and dropped my gloves in the recycler. "I'll ping you with the results, Bernard. Stay away from those sketchy underpants, and tell what's-his-name he needs some control."

Bernard wriggled into her suit, her face pink. "Yeah. I'll do that."

"Or you can send what's-his-name here to get some advice," Onopka offered. Her grin was tight and humorless, and Bernard's only response was an upward jerk of her chin.

"All right, Specialist," I said when the door closed. "You have five minutes."

"You still not going to give me an abortion?"

"I can't," I said. "I have gone over and over the ship's laws and charters."

"Okay, no fucking around," Onopka said. "You don't give me an abortion, I'll do it myself. And I'll leave a note that says you helped. So, if something happens to me—I know it's dangerous—if something happens to me, you'll be implicated."

"Specialist Onopka, that's blackmail."

"Yes, it is. And if I continue being pregnant, and something goes wrong, you'll still be implicated." For a moment, she put her hands to her face, nails digging into her skin, knuckles white; and when she heaved a ragged sigh and looked at me again, her brow and cheekbones bore those marks like scarification.

"Not if I take careful enough notes," I said. Carelessly.

"Say that again."

"'Not if I take careful enough notes?'" Now I was the one who felt like hiding her face. "Specialist, you're asking me to falsify medical documents."

The smile on her face smoothed out the stippling from her nails. "I am asking you to make careful documentation that will cement your integrity as a caretaker of everyone on this ship. *Everyone* on this ship."

The door chirped politely: my next patient, who had an appointment for a biopsy on her cervix. "I'll think about it," I said.

"Don't think too long," Onopka said. "Time flies."

Do you know what decided me? Specialist Onopka had never given me a reason; she never offered me an excuse or justified her request. It was enough that she did not want to be pregnant. On Earth, I was required to listen to dozens of statements from women about why, why, why. Legally, they had to beg me, and their pleas had to be recorded. All of these interviews were harrowing. I had to listen to women peel open their souls and bring out their shame, their anger, their fears. It was humiliating for them, and I could never say enough times how sorry I was.

That night in our community mess, I let conversations wash over me, while beneath the surface the years of apologia roiled and muttered.

My mother never believed me—
They cut ChildRen and Infants Benefits again—
He got fired—
She got fired—
I got fired—
He said that when he got out of jail he'd sue for custody and I'd be tied to him forever—
They won't give me my meds if I'm pregnant—
There's no health care for a pregnant man—

And through it all the hiss of assault. Of violence. Whether from someone else or from one's own body.

I signed off on almost every one of those requests, and submitted my patients' tears of relief, hugs, a kind of feverish gratitude I had not remembered until now. Onopka would never ask for a hug or something to wipe her eyes. She was the kind of woman who, a century or so ago, would break off a spoke from a bicycle wheel and use it on herself. Damn the consequences.

Ah, those consequences forever damned, the future challenged, the past scorned. In looking too far forward, the crafters of Kybele law forgot to look back and see where they came from. That for every bright bolt hurled, there was an arm, an impetus, the spark of thought that engenders the end result of the blade quivering in the target. Had they chosen not to recall where each plastic fetal bag and frozen zygote originated? Or did they simply not care, so in love with potential that they valued it more than the actual?

And look at us now, my friend, still hurtling along,

physics and biology disguised as a promise. You know how it is with an idea, with a vow, don't you? Once it's realized, it no longer exists.

And that was why the next day I did the abortion for Specialist Onopka, because she and I were real, and not promises. I refused, finally, to chain her destiny to someone else's vision. A vision that had no sense of history, of origin. We star-farers have to know where we came from, if we're to survive past a promise.

Lunchtime? Oh yes, I'm allowed to eat with my visitors. The food's not wonderful, but it's sufficient in macronutrients that I'm not ill-nourished. And you can brag to your classmates you ate our food. Perhaps as your teachers if you can set up a project, a petition to get better rations for prisoners. Never forget, someday it might be you down here!

Of course, you may take a picture. Get the side with the eye socket—it's healed quite nicely.

AUTHOR BIOS

Querus Abuttu, or "Dr. Q.," writes strange dark tales, speculative fiction, and weird sci-fi. She is a midnight poet, savior of road turtles, and a solitary green-gray witch living on the wooded banks of Iron Shores. When she's not writing, Dr. Q. explores the wilds of Virginia and interviews interesting individuals for her next novel. She loves foraging for wild foods, edible landscaping, and trying to find 101 ways to thwart deer from eating her plants. You may find her in a local pub drinking non-alcoholic craft beers, talking to random people, and writing furiously in a tattered notebook that she keeps under her pillow at night. Visit her author website at QuerusAbuttu.com.

James Beamon has an unbelievable past, mostly because he uses his spare time writing down fabrications to sell to others. That said, he's been in the Air Force, to Iraq and Afghanistan, on the Nebula Recommended Reading List, and in trouble more times than he cares to honestly admit. But he doesn't even try to sell honesty, claiming it doesn't have a believable character arc. Currently he lives with his wife, son, and attack cat in Virginia and invites you all to check out what he's up to on Twitter (@WriterBeamon) or on his blog fictigristle.wordpress.com.

Zoë Brigley is a Welsh-American writer, the editor of *Poetry Wales* and poetry editor for Seren Books. She has three award-winning poetry collections, most recently *Hand & Skull* (2019), as well as a collection of nonfiction essays*: Notes from a Swing State: Writing from Wales and America* (2019).

Sarah Hans is an award-winning writer, editor, and teacher whose stories have appeared in more than 30 publications, including *Love Letters to Poe* and *Pseudopod*. She is the author of the horror novel *Entomophobia*, as well as the short story collection *Dead Girls Don't Love*. You can also find her on Twitter, Instagram, and TikTok under the handle @witchwithabook, where she loves to talk about living the spooky life. She lives in Ohio with her partner, stepdaughter, and an entirely reasonable number of pets.

Tenea D. Johnson is a multimedia storyteller, musician, editor, arts & empowerment entrepreneur, and award-winning author of 7 speculative fiction works, including 2021's releases, *Frequencies, a Fiction Album* and *Broken Fevers*, of which *Publishers Weekly* wrote "the 14 hard-hitting, memorable short stories and prose vignettes in this powerhouse collection...are astounding in their originality" (starred review). Her debut novel *Smoketown* won the Parallax Award for excellence in a speculative fiction work by a person of color while *R/evolution* earned an honorable mention that year, as well. Her short work appears in anthologies like *Mothership: Tales from Afrofuturism and Beyond, Sycorax's Daughters,* and *Blue and Gray: Ghost Stories from the Civil War*. Her musical stories were heard at venues including The Public Theater and The Knitting Factory. Her virtual home is teneadjohnson. com. Stop by anytime.

EV Knight is the author of the Bram Stoker Award-winning debut novel *The Fourth Whore*. She released her sophomore novel, *Children of Demeter*, as well as a novella, *Partum*, in 2021. Her novella *Three Days in the Pink Tower* was released in 2022, and she has stories featured in several various anthologies. EV lives in one of America's most haunted cities—Savannah, GA with her husband, her beloved Chinese Crested Gozer Augustus, and their three naughty sphynx cats.

Michelle Renee Lane holds an MFA in Writing Popular Fiction from Seton Hill University. She writes dark speculative fiction about identity politics and women of color battling their inner demons while fighting/falling in love with monsters. Her work includes elements of fantasy, horror, romance, and erotica. Her short fiction appears in the anthologies *Terror Politico: A Screaming World in Chaos, The Monstrous Feminine: Dark Tales of Dangerous Women, The Dystopian States of America, Graveyard Smash, Dead Awake, Midnight & Indigo: Twenty-Two Speculative Stories by Black Women Writers* and *The One That Got Away*, and has been featured on The Wicked Library podcast. Her Bram Stoker Award-nominated debut novel, *Invisible Chains* (2019), is available from Haverhill House Publishing. The Spanish language translation, *Cadenas Invisibles* (2022), is available from Dilatando Mentes Editorial. Her nonfiction can be found at Medium, Speculative Chic, and in *Writers Workshop of Horror 2* (2021).

Three-time Shirley Jackson Award finalist and 2020 Edgar Award-winner **Livia Llewellyn** was born in Anchorage, Alaska. Llewellyn's work has been published in *Subterranean Press, Apex Magazine*, and *The Magazine of Bizarro Fiction*, as well as anthologies like Ellen Datlow's *The Best Horror of the Year* series.

Foz Meadows is a queer Australian author, essayist, reviewer, and poet. In 2019, she won the Hugo Award for Best Fan Writer; she has also received the Norma K. Hemming Award in 2018 and the Ditmar Award for Best Fan Writer in 2017. Her essays, reviews, poetry, and short fiction have appeared in various venues, including *Uncanny Magazine, Apex Magazine, Goblin Fruit, The Huffington Post*, and *Strange Horizons*. Foz currently lives in California with her family. Her most recent novel, *A Strange and Stubborn Endurance*, is out from Tor in 2022.

A high school history and government teacher, **Donna J.W. Munro** writes dark fantasy, horror, YA, and science fiction. Munro's stories have appeared in a number of journals and anthologies, and she is the author of the YA fantasy horror book *Revelation*, the first in the Poppet Cycle novels.

Lee Murray is a writer, editor, screenwriter, and poet from Aotearoa, New Zealand. She is a four-time Bram Stoker Awards® winner, Shirley Jackson Award winner, and a USA Today Bestselling author. Read more at www.leemurray.info.

Born and raised on the Great Plains, **Marguerite Reed** worked for over a decade in the most notorious abortion clinic in the United States. That experience, as well as that of serving as a landed Baroness in the SCA, has provided a plethora of research opportunities. Her work has appeared in *Strange Horizons, Lone Star Stories, Weird Tales*, and twice received Honorable Mention in Gardner Dozois' *The Year's Best Science Fiction*. Her first novel, *Archangel*, won the Philip K Dick Special Citation in 2016. Currently, she is at work on a fantasy novel while living in Kansas with her husband, two children, and a remarkably cranky calico cat.

Marsheila (Marcy) Rockwell is an award-nominated tie-in writer and poet. Her work includes the novels *Marvel Untold: Sisters of Sorcery,* SF/H thriller *7 SYKOS*, and *The Shard Axe* series, set in the world of Dungeons & Dragons Online, as well as dozens of short stories, poems, and comic book scripts. She is a disabled pediatric cancer/mental health awareness advocate and a reconnecting Chippewa/Métis. She lives in the Valley of the Sun with her husband, three of their five children, two rescue kitties (one from hell), and far too many books. You can find out more here: marsheilarockwell.com.

Rebecca Rowland is the American author of *The Horrors Hiding in Plain Sight, Pieces, Shagging the Boss,* and *Optic Nerve,* and the curator of six horror anthologies, including the bestseller *Unburied: A Collection of Queer Dark Fiction.* Her short stories and guest essays regularly appear in a variety of publications and horror websites, and she occasionally reviews fiction collections for Scotland's Ginger Nuts of Horror. She is an Active member of the Horror Writers Association, adores cats, vodka martinis, and cheese plates (in that order), and loves to entertain visitors at her website, RowlandBooks.com. Follow her on Instagram @Rebecca_Rowland_books.

Sumiko Saulson is an award-winning author of Afro-surrealist and multicultural sci-fi and horror, whose latest novel, *Happiness and Other Diseases,* is available on Mocha Memoirs Press. Winner of the HWA Scholarship from Hell (2016), BCC Voice "Reframing the Other" contest (2017), Mixy Award (2017), Afrosurrealist Writer Award (2018), HWA Diversity Grant (2020), and Ladies of Horror Fiction Grant (2021). Sumiko has an AA in English from Berkeley City College, writes a column called "Writing While Black" for a national Black newspaper, the San Francisco BayView, is the host of the SOMA Leather and LGBT Cultural District's "Erotic Storytelling Hour," and teaches courses at the Speculative Fiction Academy.

Lynne Schmidt is the granddaughter of a Holocaust survivor, and mental health professional with a focus in trauma and healing. She is the winner of the 2020 New Women's Voices Contest and author of the chapbooks *Dead Dog Poems* (forthcoming from Finishing Line Press), *Gravity* (Nightingale and Sparrow Press), which was listed as one of the 17 Best Breakup Books to Read in 2020, and *On Becoming a Role Model* (Thirty West), which was featured on The Wardrobe's Best Dressed for PTSD Awareness Week. Her work has received the Maine Nonfiction Award, Editor's Choice Award, and was a 2018 and 2019

PNWA finalist for memoir and poetry, respectively. Lynne was a five-time 2019 and 2020 Best of the Net Nominee, and an honorable mention for the Charles Bukowski and Doug Draime Poetry Awards. In 2012, she started the project, AbortionChat, which aims to lessen the stigma around abortion. When given the choice, Lynne prefers the company of her three dogs and one cat to humans.

Marge Simon lives in Ocala, FL. She edits a column for the HWA Newsletter, "Blood & Spades: Poets of the Dark Side," and serves on the HWA Board of Trustees. She is the second woman to be acknowledged by the SF&F Poetry Association with a Grand Master Award. She has won three Bram Stoker Awards, Rhysling Awards for Best Long and Best Short Poetry, the Elgin Award for Poetry Collection, the Dwarf Stars Award, and Strange Horizons Readers' Award. Marge's poems and stories have appeared in *Asimov's SF, Silver Blade, Bête Noire, Grievous Angel, Daily Science Fiction*, and in the anthologies *You, Human, Chiral Mad*, and *The Beauty of Death*, to name a few. She attends the ICFA annually as a guest poet/writer and is on the board of the Speculative Literary Foundation.

Angela Yuriko Smith is a third-generation Shimanchu-American and an award-winning poet, author, and publisher with 20+ years of experience as a professional writer in nonfiction. Publisher of *Space & Time Magazine* (est. 1966), a two-time Bram Stoker Awards® Winner, and HWA Mentor of the Year for 2020. Connect with her at angelaysmith.com.

Mary Turzillo's "Mars Is No Place for Children" won a 1999 Nebula, and her *Lovers & Killers* won the 2013 Elgin. *Sweet Poison,* with Marge Simon, was a Stoker finalist and Elgin winner. Mary has been a British SF Association, Pushcart, Stoker, Dwarf Stars, and Rhysling finalist. *Victims* (Weasel Press), a recent poetry collection with Marge

Simon and a Stoker finalist, features themes consonant with "Crawl Space." Recently published is a more cheerful story collection, *Cosmic Cats & Fantastic Furballs* (WordFire). To release pent-up frustration at the state of women's rights, she competes internationally as a fencer. She lives in Ohio with scientist-poet-fencer Geoffrey Landis. On Mother's Day, 2022, Turzillo was the Author Guest of Honor at Marcon 2022, the biggest genre convention in Ohio, often rivaling Worldcons in its membership.

Nicole M. Wolverton is a novelist and Pushcart-nominated short story writer raised in the hinterlands of rural Pennsylvania, now living in the Philadelphia area. She is the author of *The Trajectory of Dreams* (Bitingduck Press, 2013) and editor of *Bodies Full of Burning* (Sliced Up Press, 2021). Her short fiction and creative nonfiction have appeared in nearly three dozen magazines, anthologies, and podcasts, including the *Saturday Evening Post*, *Nighty Night with Rabia Chaudry* podcast, and *Hungry Ghost Magazine*. Find her online at www.nicolewolverton.com.

ABOUT THE ARTIST

Aimee Hagerty Johnson's lifelong love of literature, art, and research is at the heart of her work as an illustrator, so every project is an excuse to read, study, and learn.

Some of her favorite things to draw are lived-in landscapes, interesting faces, and timeworn objects (also, fanny packs). Her illustrations are created using gouache, ink, acrylic, watercolor pencil, and watercolor pastels on paper, canvas, or wood. Aimee's illustrations and writing appear in magazines such as *Taproot, Highlights Hello, Ladybug, Root and Star, Spider*, and *Honest History*. She earned a BFA in Illustration from the Minneapolis College of Art and Design. Aimee works from her studio in beautiful Northfield, Minnesota.

ABOUT THE EDITORS

E.F. Schraeder

E.F. Schraeder is a rustbelt writer and librarian who believes in ghosts, magic, and dogs. The author of *As Fast as She Can* (Sirens Call Publications, 2022), the Imadjinn Award finalist *Liar: Memoir of a Haunting* (Omnium Gatherum, 2021), and other works, Schraeder's short fiction, poetry, and nonfiction work has also appeared in a number of anthologies and journals. Schraeder earned an interdisciplinary Ph.D. emphasizing social philosophy and holds advanced degrees in Library Science and applied ethics.

Elaine Schleiffer

Elaine Schleiffer is a community organizer and advocate based in Cleveland, Ohio who focuses on healthcare access, public safety, and education. She is a former board chair at Preterm and has testified in front of the Ohio legislature about several iterations of anti-abortion bills, and her path toward advocating for reproductive rights began with her first abortion many years ago. She is the author of *Our House on the Sand* (Crisis Chronicles Press, 2019) and editor of *Recording Corona* (Purple Palm Press, 2020).